NADIA ISLAM, ON THE RECORD

NADIA ISLAM, ON THE RECORD

WORDS BY:
ADIBA JAIGIRDAR

ART BY:
AVANI DWIVEDI

Quill Tree Books
An Imprint of HarperCollinsPublishers

HarperCollins Children's Books,
a division of HarperCollins Publishers,
195 Broadway, New York, NY 10007

HarperCollins Publishers, Macken House,
39/40 Mayor Street Upper, Dublin 1, D01 C9W8, Ireland

Quill Tree Books is an imprint of HarperCollins Publishers.

ISBN 978-0-06-328598-9

Typography by Laura Mock
25 26 27 28 29 LBC 5 4 3 2 1

First Edition

For my siblings,
Shafqat Ahrar and Labiba

NADIA ISLAM,
ON THE RECORD

Nadia Is Not Excited for Summer Vacation

It was the last week of school, but Nadia Islam was not looking forward to the upcoming summer vacation.

"What if we went to Bangladesh *after* Ramadan?" Nadia asked, glancing out the car window instead of at her ammu in the driver's seat. She didn't want to see Ammu's unhappy face—the one she'd had for this past month whenever Nadia brought up their travel plans. It came with her usual scrunched-up eyebrows and downturned lips. Nadia did not like her ammu's unhappy face at all.

"Nadia, I'm sorry, but . . . we've already booked the tickets," Ammu said.

"We could change the tickets!" Nadia said. How

1

much could it cost to change the date to later in the summer? No big deal at all. But what Ammu was asking Nadia to do was a *huge* deal. She and her best friend, Yasmin, had been looking forward to spending their first Ramadan together, fasting with each other, having iftar together. They'd had it all planned out . . . and then Ammu shared the news about going to Bangladesh, and it was all ruined in an instant!

"You know that's not possible," Ammu said with a sigh as she pulled the car into park in front of Nadia's school.

"Yeah, Nadia, we can't give up *our* vacation just because you have plans with Yasmin," Adam said from beside her, sticking out his tongue. Nadia wished that Adam was less excited about going to Bangladesh, but he basically jumped up and down with joy when he heard the news. He was excited about leaving the country and meeting the rest of their family, but Nadia felt anxious about it all. Bangladesh was just *so* far away, and she'd only ever seen her family through the tiny screen of Ammu's phone.

"Be good, both of you," Ammu said, glancing back from the driver's seat. "No teasing, Adam. And Nadia . . . you and Yasmin can still support each other through Ramadan. You won't even notice a difference."

But Ammu didn't get it—it wouldn't be the same at all. Nadia wanted to sulk in the back seat of the car, but she knew it wouldn't change Ammu's mind.

So, she just said, "Okay," even though it didn't feel fair and the last thing Nadia wanted to do was tell Yasmin the bad news. Nadia and Adam got out of the car and strapped on their backpacks. Nadia's backpack felt as heavy as her disappointment about her conversation with Ammu.

"Race you to the front door?" Adam asked, almost like he knew a good race would put Nadia in a better mood.

That perked Nadia right up. She didn't even respond; she just ran, her backpack loudly jingling behind her. She touched the glass of the front

doors a minute later. She had won!

"You lose!" Nadia said, even while gasping for air.

"No fair, you cheated," Adam said through huffs of breath as he came to a stop beside her.

Nadia just shrugged. All was fair in their competitions; Adam should have known that by now.

Yasmin was already sitting at her desk in their class-room when Nadia arrived. Yasmin's eyes snapped up, like she could sense Nadia. Nadia waved, hurrying over to her own desk beside Yasmin's.

Ever since their first-grade teacher, Mrs. Waldroop, had assigned Yasmin to sit next to Nadia, they'd been best friends. And every single year, they'd beg to be seated next to each other, promising that they'd never get into any trouble. It helped that everyone loved Yasmin since she was such a stickler for the rules. If there was a rule to be followed, Yasmin would follow it. Nadia wasn't quite such a rule follower, but she guessed it was their differences that made them such good friends.

"Did you convince her?" Yasmin asked, hope bright in her eyes. Nadia had told her last night about her plans to beg Ammu to postpone their trip until the end of Ramadan.

Nadia shook her head sadly. It had been her last chance—and it hadn't worked.

"I guess we really won't be spending our first Ramadan fasting together, even though our parents said that we would," Nadia said. The two of them had made so many plans and now none of them would happen. They were going to try out new

5

recipes together for iftar, they were going to recite the Qur'an together, and they'd even made a list of the surahs they were planning to learn during Ramadan.

Nadia wished that her parents had let her fast last year, but their rule was that both Adam and Nadia could start fasting when they were eight years old. So, Adam got to fast last year and act like he was all grown up because of it, and Nadia was left out. And even though Nadia would be able to fast this year, not fasting with Yasmin still felt like she was missing out.

To Nadia's surprise, Yasmin didn't look as sad about things as Nadia felt. She was biting her lip, like she was deep in thought.

"It's not going to be so bad, you know. I mean, it'll be kind of cool to be in Bangladesh, right?" Yasmin asked.

Nadia couldn't believe it—Yasmin sounded just like Ammu.

"But we're going to be apart for the whole

summer!" Nadia said to Yasmin.

"We can video chat each other all the time," Yasmin suggested. "So it'll be like we *are* spending our summer together."

"It won't be the same, and you know it." Nadia sighed. She wished she could feel more excited about traveling to Bangladesh. If only she could take Yasmin with her.

The bell rang, and Ms. Johnson walked into the classroom, beaming at everyone. It may have been the last week of school, but Nadia knew Ms. Johnson wasn't about to let this last week of teaching go to waste.

"Are you ready to present your projects?" Ms. Johnson asked, clapping her hands together.

Their last project of the year was all about climate change. Just last week, Ms. Johnson had taken them on a field trip to the science museum in the next town over. They'd learned all kinds of things: different ways to harness energy and how to reduce, reuse, recycle. Afterward, Ms. Johnson had put them into pairs and given each group a topic to research and present in class.

"Yes, we're ready!" Nadia and her classmates responded.

"Let's see, who to pick first . . ." Ms. Johnson said, her eyes roaming around the class. "How about Olivia and Toby?"

Olivia and Toby walked up to the front of the classroom. They had a huge poster with different pictures cut and pasted together. Their topic was renewable energy.

They put their poster on the whiteboard with some tape and began their presentation.

"Renewable energy is energy that can be naturally replaced. There are a lot of examples of renewable energy," Olivia said. She pointed to one of the pictures on her poster. "This is a windmill and it creates something called wind energy. The fans of the windmill turn and make the energy from the wind, so it's natural! And then we can use this energy for electricity."

"And this is a solar panel," Toby said, pointing to another image on the poster. "It makes energy from the sun! We can put the solar panel on the roofs of our houses, and then we don't even have to pay for electricity anymore!"

Everyone clapped at the end of Toby and Olivia's presentation.

"Good job, guys," Ms. Johnson said, joining in. She glanced over at Nadia and added, "Next, let's have Yasmin and Nadia."

Nadia and Yasmin didn't have a big poster, exactly, but they had a chart that Yasmin had drawn. She taped it up on the board. Their project was all about water.

"Yasmin and I learned during our field trip how important water conservation is," Nadia began. "That means that we need to use less water, because processing water so it's safe to use takes up a lot of energy that we should try to save!"

"We asked our families about how much water they use daily," Yasmin said, pointing to her chart.

She had drawn a few different things: There were glasses of water, some small bottles, and then one giant bottle. "In my family, my dad uses the least amount of water, my mom uses a little bit more than him, and . . . I use the most! I like to take really long showers."

"And in my family, my brother uses the least amount of water, then it's me, my dad, and finally my mom," Nadia said, pointing to each of the pictures Yasmin had drawn to show the amount of water each family member used. "Now that we know how much water we each use, next we wanted to come up with ways we could use less water."

"I'm definitely going to be taking shorter showers," Yasmin said with a nod. "And I'm always going to turn the tap off when I'm brushing my teeth."

"I'm going to do the same!" Nadia said. "And my mom promised she would take fewer baths and shorter showers *and* that she would use a watering can to water our garden, instead of the gardening hose."

"If we all figure out how much water we use and how we use it, it's a lot easier to try and use less water," Yasmin added.

Nadia nodded in agreement. "It's something we can all do for water conservation!"

Everyone clapped loudly at the end of their presentation too, and Nadia felt proud as she went back to her desk. She and Yasmin were the best team. With Yasmin's creative skills and Nadia's journalism, they were unstoppable.

"Those were some excellent presentations," Ms. Johnson said once the last team wrapped up. "I'm so proud of everything that you learned and shared about climate change. I know we're all excited about the summer vacation, but let's not forget all we've learned this year during the next few months, okay?"

"Okay, Ms. Johnson," they all called back. Nadia definitely would be more careful about how she used water after her project; she wasn't just saying it because she wanted to have the best project out of everyone.

"Now that you're all expert researchers, I have an exciting update for those of you who want to keep reporting on important issues. Next year, you're all going to be fourth graders. That means you'll be more mature, and you'll have more responsibilities. One of those responsibilities is the school newspaper."

Nadia felt her heartbeat pick up with excitement. She had been looking forward to fourth grade for this exact reason: It was fourth and fifth graders who put the school newspaper together, and Nadia had always dreamed of working on it. One day, she was going to work for a big newspaper, but for now she had to get started with the *Sweetside Elementary School Newspaper*.

She shared an excited look with Yasmin, who had wanted to work on the art section for forever. If Yasmin and Nadia were both accepted into the school newspaper, they could be working side by side next year!

"This year the school newspaper is looking for writers, editors, and artists, as well as an editor in chief. After the summer, you can each submit your work to me and Mr. McGrane, and we'll review everyone's work and select the people we think are right for the jobs. I hope you're all up for the challenge," Ms. Johnson said.

Nadia's eyes widened. She couldn't believe it— they were looking for an editor in chief! Nadia had thought that maybe she could be one of writers for the newspaper next year, covering the stories of school picture day or investigating why Mrs. Waldroop always wore a scarf to school, even when it was hot. She had never imagined becoming the editor in chief, but maybe this was her chance.

All she had to do was come up with the perfect news story.

Nadia Prepares for Her Greatest Adventure Yet

As Nadia and Yasmin walked from school that day, they couldn't stop talking about the newspaper.

"You're going to be just like Millie Davies next year!" Yasmin said. Millie was the current editor in chief of the school newspaper, and Nadia and Yasmin were obsessed with her. She was the coolest fifth grader that Nadia had ever met (maybe even one of the coolest people she had ever met). She was always nice to Nadia and Yasmin even though she was way older than they were.

Millie had been the person to start the Interview with a Teacher section in their school newspaper last year so that every edition of the paper now featured a brand-new interview with one of the teachers from Sweetside Elementary. Nadia only dreamed of doing something amazing and creative just like Millie!

"If I want to be like Millie, I have to come up with a really good article to submit!" Nadia said. She wished more than ever that she was staying home this summer. Then, she and Yasmin would have all the time in the world to brainstorm together and come up with the best newspaper article ever!

Yasmin scrunched up her eyebrows like she always did when she was deep in thought. Nadia was excited—maybe Yasmin would already have an idea for it.

"You could write all about the things you see in Bangladesh!" Yasmin said excitedly. "Nobody will expect an article about Bangladesh. Most of them don't know anything about it!"

Nadia's heart sank at the suggestion. *She* barely knew anything about Bangladesh. She didn't want to spend the summer there *and* write about it. She was sure that nobody would be interested, especially since nobody even knew where Bangladesh was!

"I don't know," Nadia said. "Maybe I could talk to Khalamoni and ask for her advice."

Nadia called her aunt, Ammu's younger sister, Khalamoni. Khalamoni worked for a big national newspaper and wrote about all kinds of things. Khalamoni was Nadia's inspiration for being a journalist. She always shared stories of her research, interviews, and writing with Nadia. Now, Nadia finally had the chance to do her own research, her own interviews, and her own writing. She had to take it seriously, and she knew that Khalamoni would help her figure out exactly what she needed to do.

"That's a good idea!" Yasmin said. She had only met Khalamoni once, a few months ago, when Khalamoni had been working on a story nearby. Yasmin and her parents had come over for dinner, like they sometimes did, and Khalamoni had told everyone about a feature she was writing about a couple in town who had decided to get married at the age of one hundred! Nadia couldn't believe it. She was only eight years old, so she couldn't imagine being one hundred!

"You could ask her about the Bangladesh idea," Yasmin added.

Nadia nodded, though she still wasn't sure she liked *that* idea. "Or I could also ask her about writing about my first Ramadan," Nadia said, the idea suddenly appearing in her mind like a light switch being turned on. "How we have to fast from dawn to dusk, the foods that we eat at sehri and iftar, even those surahs I hear Ammu and Abbu say before they break their fast!"

Yasmin nodded her head fast, like she couldn't agree with Nadia more. "Maybe you could even include some things about Ramadan for Nigerians. Like the foods that *we* eat."

Nadia liked that idea a lot. The job of a journalist

was more than just reporting on one experience. She could already imagine Khalamoni's eyes lighting up when she told her about this idea. But she wondered if it would be enough for her to get the editor in chief position.

"What are you going to submit to the newspaper?" Nadia asked Yasmin. Yasmin might not want to be editor in chief, but Nadia knew she would blow the teachers away with her amazing art!

"Hmm, I'm not sure," Yasmin said, looking thoughtful. "I want to make something special to submit. Maybe I can draw something to do with my summer too, even if it won't be as exciting as yours."

Nadia wasn't so sure how exciting her summer was going to be, but she nodded in agreement just the same.

Suddenly, Adam pushed in between Nadia and Yasmin, like the annoying brother he often was. "What are you two talking about?"

"Nadia and I are both going to work for the school newspaper next year! And Nadia is going to be the new editor in chief!" Yasmin declared proudly.

"If Ms. Johnson and Mr. McGrane like the story I submit at the start of school next year," Nadia said. She didn't want to be too confident about her story before she'd even come up with the idea. And definitely not before she spoke to Khalamoni. She was afraid she would jinx the whole thing.

"You're going to be doing work during the summer vacation?" Adam asked, wrinkling his nose up. "What about Ramadan? And playing video games together?"

"You don't even know that Nanu's house *has* any video games to play," Nadia pointed out.

"Don't your cousins live with your grand-mother?" Yasmin asked. "I bet they have games, if they're anything like your family."

Nadia wasn't sure. She knew that the Islams loved games, whether it was video games, board games, or anything else. Nadia and Adam had game nights every month with Abbu and Ammu, where they would play Snakes and Ladders, or Mario Kart, or even Pictionary. Abbu and Ammu loved games and competition just as much as Adam and Nadia. Sometimes Yasmin and her family even joined them on their game nights, though they weren't as competitive as Nadia's family. Yasmin's parents liked spending game night talking about politics and trading Bengali and Nigerian recipes more than they liked playing games!

"I'm going to ask Ammu if I can bring our Nintendo to Bangladesh," Adam said in a worried voice. Adam had never gone a whole summer without playing Mario Kart. Nadia hoped their family in Bangladesh also liked games. Otherwise, who would they even play Mario Kart with?

Nadia and Adam waved goodbye to Yasmin at the crossroads near their house before walking the rest of the way home. Nadia couldn't believe that it was almost the end of the school year, and Ramadan was just around the corner.

The house was chaos when Nadia and Adam opened the front door. There was a big suitcase open right in front of the entrance, with half of it filled with candy! Big bars of chocolate and bags full of Nadia's favorite sweets. But there was also a bunch of clothes strewn on top of the half-packed suitcase, like someone had forgotten them there. Abbu was on the phone, having a loud conversation in Bangla, while Ammu walked toward Nadia armed with a stack of clothes so high that Nadia could only make out the top of her head.

"Nadia! Adam!" Ammu said, peeking out from behind her stack of clothes. "How was school? Were you two okay walking home?"

"Yes," Nadia and Adam said in unison, sharing a worried look between them.

When Ammu said they had to pack for Bangladesh this week, Nadia hadn't expected so much messiness. She wanted to tell Ammu about how

Ms. Johnson had said they were looking for an editor in chief for the school newspaper. And how Nadia was going to write something to get the job. She was going to ask about calling Khalamoni so Nadia could brainstorm ideas with her. But seeing all the chaos, she wasn't sure if it was the right time.

"School was okay. Ms. Johnson loved our presentation about water conservation," Nadia added.

"I'm glad!" Ammu said. "I know you and Yasmin worked very hard on that project."

"And Ms. Marsh asked us all to write short stories about our dream summer vacation. We had to use a lot of descriptive language," Adam said.

"I hope you wrote all about Bangladesh," Ammu said.

Adam nodded, but Nadia knew he wasn't telling the truth. He had his arms crossed behind his back, like he always did when he lied.

If Nadia's Khalamoni were here, she would have asked Adam a few more questions, to get to the bottom of Adam's short story. A journalist always questioned everything, according to Khalamoni. They even questioned people's questions sometimes.

"What did you write about Bangladesh?" Nadia asked, turning to Adam with her hands on her hips.

"Um, about . . . mangoes," Adam said, nodding. "I love mangoes and in my short story I was eating all the delicious Bangladeshi mangoes."

Nadia had to admit, that was a pretty good lie.

"The mangoes in Bangladesh *are* the best mangoes in the world," Ammu said. She had a faraway look in her eyes, like she could see Bangladeshi mango trees somewhere in the distance.

According to Yasmin, Nigerian mangoes were the best in the world. Nadia wasn't sure who was being factual about it: Yasmin or Ammu. She had a feeling it was neither.

"Exactly, and that's why it's my dream summer vacation," Adam said triumphantly.

"Well, soon it'll be your *real* summer vacation,"

Ammu said, finally plopping down her stack of clothes into the open suitcase. "I put suitcases in both of your rooms. Do you think you can start packing?"

"Yes!" Adam said. He ran into the sitting room, grabbed the Nintendo, and disappeared into his bedroom.

Ammu shook her head. "I'll have to take that Nintendo out of his suitcase later."

"Why are you bringing so much candy?" Nadia asked, inspecting all the packets in between Ammu's clothes.

"They don't have these in Bangladesh," Ammu said, picking up one of the bags filled with a variety of Nadia's favorite candy. "I thought your cousins might like them. And your Khalamoni asked me to buy some extra on her behalf since she can't go shopping before the flight."

"Khalamoni is coming to Bangladesh too?" Nadia asked. She could feel a seed of excitement in her stomach. It was the first time she'd felt excited about this trip since Ammu and Abbu had announced they'd be spending the summer in Bangladesh last month.

"Oh . . . didn't I tell you?" Ammu frowned down at Nadia. She'd been so busy in the past month that every time Nadia tried to speak to her, Ammu was completely distracted. Most of the time, she was on the phone to her family and friends in Bangladesh to tell them that they would be coming soon, or she was out shopping for presents. "Yes, your Khalamoni said she was researching an article to do with Bangladesh, so she decided she would fly there with us!"

It had been a few weeks since Nadia had seen Khalamoni. Khalamoni lived only an hour away and visited them as often as she could, but she traveled a lot for work, which meant that she never had a set schedule. But no matter what, she always made sure to make time for them during the important occasions, like every Eid and all the birthdays.

"Why is she traveling all the way to Bangladesh to write her article?" Nadia asked.

"Oh, I guess it's been a while since you and Khalamoni spoke," Ammu said, looking thoughtful. "Your khalamoni is doing some freelance journalism, and her first article is going to be something about Bangladesh."

Nadia's eyes widened. Khalamoni had told her about how sometimes her newspaper would get article pitches from a freelancer. But she had never mentioned wanting to be a freelance journalist!

"What's her article about?" Nadia asked.

"You'll have to ask her that, Nadia. Now, come on. We have to get packing if we want to be ready for our flight tomorrow morning," Ammu said, clapping her hands together.

Nadia knew that meant Ammu wanted to wrap up this conversation and concentrate. She weaved past the suitcase and Abbu (who was still on the phone) and into her own bedroom, where Ammu had left her Minnie Mouse suitcase. She had a lot of packing to do, but Nadia was beginning to get excited about her trip. It wasn't the summer that Nadia had wanted, but maybe this could be even better. After all, not everybody had the best journalist ever as their aunt. And maybe Nadia could do some real-life journalism with Khalamoni at her side.

She opened up her suitcase and began to put away her clothes, ready for the adventure ahead of her.

NADIA ISLAM'S INVESTIGATIVE QUESTIONS ABOUT BANGLADESH

<u>Question #1</u>: In Bangladesh, I have lots of family members! My mom's brother, who I call Mama. His wife, who I call Mami. Their daughters, Lily and Rosie, and my grandmother, who I call Nanu. But what are they really like? And do they like playing games as much as me and Adam?

<u>Question #2</u>: Summer in our town is hot but not *too* hot, and it's usually sunny! What is summer in Bangladesh like?

<u>Question #3</u>: We have to get on a plane and fly for a *long* time to get to Bangladesh from the USA. How long does it take to get to Bangladesh?!

Nadia Goes on the Longest Flight in the History of the World

Nadia hated the airport. There were too many people, and too much noise, and Ammu and Abbu were too stressed out the entire time.

They all waited in the long line to check in their luggage. Nadia and Adam tried to see who could lift the heaviest bag. Nadia's Minnie Mouse suitcase was the easiest to lift, but Ammu's suitcase, filled with all her candy, presents, and clothes, was the heaviest. Even Abbu could barely lift that one.

"We're tied!" Nadia declared when neither she nor Adam could lift it even an inch off the ground.

"We have to have another competition to figure out a winner," Adam said.

After checking in their bags and going through

security, Nadia and her family sat down at the seats by the gate. Nadia hated the seats there; they were cold and uncomfortable. She hoped that the seats on their flight would be much nicer.

"How much time does it take to get to Bangladesh?" Nadia asked, taking out her sparkly purple notebook so she could jot down the answer. Being a journalist meant always asking questions and always taking notes. How else would Nadia remember all the correct facts?

"Well, let's see," Ammu said, taking out their boarding passes. "It's a twelve-and-a-half-hour flight to Dubai."

A twelve-and-a-half-hour flight! What was Nadia supposed to do for twelve and a half hours? Still, she wrote it down in her notebook. She couldn't wait to share this information with Yasmin.

"And then . . . five hours from Dubai to Dhaka," Ammu continued. Nadia wrote that down too. Five hours wasn't too bad, but it was still long!

"And another hour from Dhaka to Sylhet," Ammu finished. Even she looked worried about the long journey ahead.

"I'm already tired!" Adam groaned. They'd had to wake up extra early to come to the airport right on time.

"You can sleep once we get on the flight," Abbu said. "We should be boarding soon."

The seats around them at the gate were slowly filling up, and Nadia looked everywhere, hoping that Khalamoni would suddenly appear.

"Where is she?" Nadia groaned. She had so many questions for Khalamoni.

"She'll be here soon, Nadia," Ammu said with a sigh. "But remember, it's a long journey for her too. Keep your questions to a minimum."

"A minimum?"

"That just means . . . not too many questions!" Ammu said.

Nadia wrote down the word *minimum* and Ammu's definition right beside it. Sometimes, being a journalist meant having to know a lot of different words. That's why Nadia kept her own dictionary of new words in the back of her notebook.

When Nadia looked up, she finally spotted Khalamoni walking toward their seats at the airport gate. She was Ammu's younger sister, and she looked similar to Ammu. She had a perfectly oval face, brown eyes shaped like half moons, and skin the color of a sandy beach on a hot summer day. Today, she wore a pair of black jeans and a pink button-up blouse.

"Assalam alaikum!" Khalamoni said, stopping in front of Nadia and her family. She blinked slowly, like she was tired, and put down the cup of coffee she was holding on the chair next to Nadia. Ammu stood up as soon as Khalamoni arrived and pulled her into a hug. Khalamoni gave Abbu a nod and a smile and ruffled Adam's hair in greeting before picking up her coffee cup and sitting down right next to Nadia.

"What are you writing?" Khalamoni asked as her way of greeting. A flutter of excitement rose in Nadia's chest. She'd been waiting to tell Khalamoni all about the school newspaper and applying to be editor in chief.

"All about our journey to Bangladesh," Nadia said. "I'm trying to write down all the important things, so I remember, and all the questions that I have. Just like a real journalist might."

Khalamoni smiled wide, like she was proud of Nadia, and the flutter of excitement in Nadia's chest grew.

"So, you're planning to do some journalism during your summer vacation?" Khalamoni asked curiously. "I wouldn't have been caught dead doing any work when I was on a school vacation."

This was the moment Nadia had been waiting for. She took a deep breath before the excited words burst out of her.

"I'm going apply to be editor in chief of my school newspaper!" she exclaimed.

Khalamoni smiled wide.

"Editor in chief? That will be amazing, Nadia!" she said, like she was prouder of Nadia than she had ever been. Nadia smiled back.

"But I have to write a really good article so that my teachers can see I'd be the best editor in chief ever!" Nadia said. She didn't mention Millie and how good of an editor in chief *she* was.

"Nadia is *so* boring!" Adam declared, poking Nadia in the shoulder. "All she talks about is the school newspaper and journalism! I'm not doing any work during *my* summer vacation."

"Hey!" Nadia cried, poking him right back. He shot her a glare, and she stuck out her tongue.

"Okay, okay. Enough," Abbu said, rubbing the

space between his eyebrows like he always did when Nadia and Adam got into a fight.

"I don't think it's boring," Khalamoni whispered to Nadia after a few moments. Like it was their own little secret. "I'll be doing journalism over the summer too, you know."

"Ammu told me!" Nadia said, excited to be clued in to Khalamoni's journalist secrets. "She said you were going to be a freelance journalist, and that you were writing a special article."

Khalamoni nodded. "I thought I would have more freedom to write about the things I care about without being tied to one paper."

Nadia wrinkled her eyebrows, confused. She thought that journalists could just write about what they wanted. Wasn't being a journalist about reporting the truth and sharing facts?

"Why didn't you have freedom to write about what you wanted before?" Nadia asked. "You didn't want to write about all those news stories you've shared with me?"

Khalamoni sighed. "A lot of them I did care

about and wanted to write about. But when you work for a big newspaper, sometimes they only care about stories that they think people will want to read. That means some stories might not get told. But . . . I want to tell those stories and report on those facts."

Nadia had never realized that even journalists might not get to report *all* the facts or write about *everyone's* stories.

"So, what's the story you want to write about in Bangladesh?" Nadia asked. She knew it had to be an important story if it made Khalamoni want to leave the big newspaper and become a freelance journalist!

"Well, I reached out to schedule an interview with this family in Bangladesh," Khalamoni said. An interview! Nadia could already imagine her khalamoni asking the difficult questions. Though Nadia wasn't really sure yet what the difficult questions *were*.

"What kind of an interview?" Nadia asked.

"There's a big climate change problem in the world, but especially in Bangladesh. And this family is doing some amazing things to help," Khalamoni explained. "I pitched a newspaper to do an article on it, and they said they were interested. So I have some time to interview them, do some research, and write a really good article. I'm hoping that if it's good enough, they'll make it into a big feature, maybe even put it on the front page since climate change is such an important issue."

"Wow!" Nadia exclaimed in awe. Khalamoni hadn't been on the front page of the papers before, even though she'd been a journalist for as long as Nadia had known her. She had done some amazing interviews and written important articles. Sometimes, Ammu read them out to Nadia and Adam at the dinner table, beaming with pride that it was her sister who was reporting real issues. Nadia felt pride too, and she shared some of her favorite articles with Yasmin. She had even saved a few of the newspaper clippings for one of her notebooks. She knew one day that would be her.

Nadia had more questions, but just then the flight attendant declared that it was time to board the plane. Nadia and her family each grabbed their hand luggage and rolled it to the front of the line. The flight attendant smiled as Nadia passed her by. They walked down a long corridor and right onto the plane.

"Our seats are this way. . . ." Abbu said, leading the whole family down the long aisle. There were already so many people here. Nadia had been on planes once or twice before, but never one this big, and she had definitely never been on a twelve-hour flight before.

Finally, Abbu stopped in front of their seats. There were three seats on the left aisle, and two in the middle.

"I want the window seat!" Adam declared before they even had a chance to sit down.

"No, I want the window seat!" Nadia protested.

"Too bad, I said I wanted it first," Adam said. And before Nadia could say much more, he slid right into the left aisle seats and plopped down on the window seat. Turning around, he stuck his tongue out at Nadia to declare his victory.

"Ammu!" Nadia cried. It wasn't fair that Adam would get the window seat just because he was fast.

Ammu sighed and shook her head, while Abbu put their luggage into the overhead lockers, like he wasn't even paying attention.

"Adam, you can have the window seat for this flight. But on the one from Dubai, it's Nadia who gets it," Ammu said sternly. It was the voice she used when she didn't want Adam and Nadia to talk back to her. It was rare for Ammu to use this voice, because most of the time she didn't mind if Adam and Nadia asked questions. But this voice meant no questions and definitely no complaints.

"Okay, Ammu," Adam said with a nod, and even though Nadia wasn't happy about it, she nodded too.

"You can sit next to me, Nadia," Khalamoni said, nodding at the two seats in the middle aisle. "And you can tell me more about your plans for this summer."

"Really?" Nadia asked excitedly. Sitting next to Khalamoni was second best to having the window seat. And this way, she wouldn't even have to deal with Adam being annoying during the entire flight.

"Really!" said Khalamoni.

The two of them slid into the middle aisle, side by side. Nadia couldn't believe she had an entire twelve-hour flight to tell Khalamoni about her summer project and ask her all the questions she wanted. Being on the longest flight in the world might not be so bad!

Nadia Visits Bangladesh
for the First Time Ever

While Adam was glued to the window, watching the clouds outside, Nadia decided to use her time next to Khalamoni properly. She told Khalamoni about all of her ideas for the school newspaper.

"Yasmin said that maybe I could write about my time in Bangladesh, but I don't think anybody would be interested in that," Nadia said honestly. She knew she could trust Khalamoni with all her thoughts and she would never judge Nadia. "I thought that maybe I could write about my first time ever fasting during Ramadan, but I don't know . . . last year, Millie did an amazing interview with Mrs. Waldroop for her article, and not only did she become editor in chief, but now they do an interview with a teacher for every edition of the school newspaper!"

Nadia wanted to do something that would have just as much of an impact as Millie's idea, but she didn't know what that was.

"Hmm," Khalamoni said. Her eyebrows were scrunched up like she was thinking really hard. "First, you should think about what kind of an article you want to write. Do you want to do an interview, like the last editor in chief? Or a feature, where you present facts but also share your own view? Or an editorial, which is all your opinion?"

Nadia had never really thought about how there were different types of writing when it came to journalism. She'd thought it was all about asking the right questions and reporting the facts!

"What kind of articles do you write?" Nadia asked.

"Well, for this climate change piece, it's going to be a feature. I'm going to interview this family, but I'm also going to do my own research about climate change in Bangladesh and what activists are doing to help. And I'm even going to add in my own perspective as a writer and someone who has lived in Bangladesh," Khalamoni explained.

Nadia thought that sounded like a *lot* of work. When Millie had done her interview with Mrs. Waldroop, it was just a question and answer! But maybe that's exactly what Nadia needed. She needed to show her teachers that she could do something that nobody at the newspaper had done yet!

"I want to write a feature too!" Nadia said excitedly.

Khalamoni beamed at Nadia. "I guess we can both work on our features together."

"Yes, yes, yes!" Nadia said. She could feel the excitement bubbling from her stomach through her whole body. With Khalamoni by her side, Nadia knew that she could write a great article and become editor in chief!

* * *

Even though the flight was *long*, it went by faster than Nadia expected. She talked to Khalamoni all about journalism, and then the two of them decided to watch episodes of Nadia's favorite TV show together. Before Nadia knew it they were boarding their second flight from Dubai where she was so tired that she fell asleep quickly.

It was only when they were a few minutes away from landing that Adam shook Nadia awake.

"Are we there yet?" Nadia mumbled, rubbing sleep out of her eyes and blinking awake.

"Almost! Look out the window," Khalamoni said excitedly from beside Adam. Her eyes were bloodshot, like she hadn't gotten much sleep at all. Nadia leaned forward toward the window. Outside, the fluffy white clouds were almost within reach. If only Nadia could open the window and touch them. But she knew from school that clouds were made of nothing but water.

Just then, the plane slanted slightly. It was going

44

to land soon! And Nadia could see cities sprawling out under their plane. It was Bangladesh!

"Wow," Nadia said. She wasn't sure what she had expected Bangladesh to look like, but it wasn't like anything she had ever imagined. There was so much green everywhere, and so much water weaving through the greenery and the cities.

Beside her, Adam craned his neck to look over Nadia. It was his first time seeing Bangladesh too.

"It's beautiful, right?" Khalamoni asked. She was peeking over Nadia's shoulders and there was a weird expression on her face. Almost like she had missed Bangladesh. It was strange because Khalamoni never really spoke about Bangladesh with Nadia. Neither did her Ammu or Abbu. But they must have loved it if they wanted to spend a whole summer here. Nadia didn't really understand it, but maybe that was because she hadn't asked the right questions.

"It is. I didn't know Bangladesh was so green!" Nadia replied.

"I didn't know that Bangladesh had so much water!" Adam added.

"Well, you know we have the green on our flag because of how much greenery there is on our land," Khalamoni said with a smile. "And we have hundreds of rivers in Bangladesh."

Nadia dug into the pocket of the seat in front of her and took out her sparkly purple notebook. She wanted to write down everything she learned during her trip.

"Maybe some of these facts will be useful for my feature article," she said to Khalamoni as she jotted down the new information. "I'm already learning a lot about Bangladesh."

"I think this summer is definitely your chance to learn a lot," Khalamoni said. And even as she smiled, there was still that weird expression on her face.

From the Dhaka airport, Nadia and her family had to get yet another plane to Sylhet. But this was their shortest flight yet. It felt to Nadia like as soon as the plane took off, it was time to land again.

The airport in Sylhet was much smaller than the one in Dhaka, even much *much* smaller than the one back home. But there were still people everywhere! When they stepped outside the airport, Nadia was surprised by how different everything felt. There was heat prickling her skin, and even the air felt a little heavier than usual. It was also weird because when they had gone to the airport back home it had been daytime . . . and after all the time flying, it was daytime here too!

"There's your mama!" Ammu said, waving at a man who was approaching them with a wide grin. Nadia had seen her uncle a few times on their computer screen when Ammu video chatted with him. She always came along with a smile to say salaam, but nothing more than that. Now he ran up to them and began hugging them one by one. First Ammu, so tightly that Nadia got a little worried. Then Khalamoni—just as tight. Then he hugged Adam, ruffling his hair as he let go. And finally, he turned to Nadia.

"Look how much our little Nadia has grown!" Mama said. He pulled her into a warm embrace, and despite the heat, Nadia didn't mind the hug at all.

After all the hugs and telling everyone just how much they'd changed, Mama brought over some trolleys for all of their luggage. Between them, they needed three for all their bags.

"I don't know how we'll fit all your things into our house," Mama joked as he took them over to his car. They piled into the car, while Mama loaded their suitcases in the back. Then they were off. They weaved through Sylhet city, past cars and houses, rickshaws and colorful little three-wheeled cars that Ammu told her were called CNGs. Nadia pressed her face to the window trying to drink it all up.

Mama said that it was only a fifteen-minute drive to their house from the airport, but there was so much traffic that it took almost twice as long for them to arrive. Nadia didn't mind so much. It gave her a chance to write down all of the things she spotted. The way the rickshaws had colorful designs with peacocks and Bangla letters, how there were colorful signs everywhere, how there were food stands selling street food on the side of the road and it made Nadia's stomach rumble.

"The place has really changed," Khalamoni commented.

"You think?" Mama asked, like he didn't quite agree.

"How did it used to be?" Nadia asked, curious.

"Hmm." Khalamoni exchanged a look with Ammu, like she wanted to make sure the both of them agreed on how things had changed. Khalamoni and Ammu had left Bangladesh within a few months of each other. Ammu because she married Abbu, and the two of them were ready to start their new life together. Khalamoni because she had gotten into her dream university. Nanu didn't mind so much because at least Ammu and Khalamoni would have each other abroad.

"Well, there used to be less traffic, definitely," Ammu said, nodding along with Khalamoni.

"And less people. Or did I just imagine that?" Khalamoni chuckled.

"Fewer cars for sure," Ammu added.

"Less noise? Less pollution?" Khalamoni said, like she wasn't sure.

Nadia had learned all about pollution in school, but when she looked outside the car window, she didn't spot any pollution. She thought pollution was supposed to look like smoke in the air, or unclean water in rivers and the sea. She hadn't spotted any of that.

"I don't see any pollution here," Nadia said.

"It's less things you can see, more what you feel or hear," Khalamoni explained. "Like the air here feels different from home, doesn't it?"

Nadia agreed that it did. It felt heavier.

"And listen to all that noise from cars and people," Mama said, rolling down his window so everyone in the car could hear the loud beeping and talking and shouting.

"That's noise pollution. It's when there's too much loud noise for a long period of time, and it can harm animals, and even people," Ammu explained.

Nadia started noting all of that down.

"Why is there more pollution now?" Nadia asked.

"Well, there are more people now, which means there are more cars," Ammu said. "And that leads to more traffic, more noise pollution, and more air pollution too from the exhausts of the cars."

"There are more factories now too. And the factories use chemicals that are bad for the environment, and that pollutes the air," Khalamoni said.

"Why don't the factories stop?" Nadia asked. "Do we have bad factories at home too?"

Khalamoni sighed. "A few, sometimes. But a lot of countries set up factories here, so they don't have to deal with the pollution. So that Bangladesh has to deal with it instead."

That didn't seem fair to Nadia. "Do they at least help Bangladesh deal with it?"

Mama scoffed, like the question was funny. "I wish, Nadia," he said.

Nadia looked outside the window again. She realized that Bangladesh didn't look like it did from up in the air. Because from above you couldn't notice all of the things Ammu and Khalamoni said had changed.

Nadia Arrives at Her Family Home

By the time they arrived at Mama's house in Sylhet, Nadia was so tired she could barely keep her eyes open. Even Adam was dozing off in his seat, half asleep and half awake.

But as Nadia and her family climbed out of the car, she rubbed her eyes and looked up at the house she would be living in all summer. It was much bigger than her house back home. A sprawling building of muted pink and white lay in front of her. Even the place where they had parked the car was massive—and like a park! Wrought iron gates closed behind them, cutting off a lot of the noise of the traffic.

"What do you think, Nadia?" Ammu asked as

she handed Nadia her suitcase.

"I can't wait to play on the swings!" Adam replied before Nadia could say anything. He pointed at the small playground to one side of the area.

"Is this whole place ours?" Nadia asked in awe.

"No, silly." Khalamoni chuckled. "It's an apartment block, like the one where you sometimes come to visit me."

"It looks different," Nadia commented. Though now that Khalamoni had pointed it out, Nadia noticed that it wasn't just *one* house; there were a few, separated by a thin area in between their walls. And Nadia supposed her whole family couldn't take up four stories.

"We grew up here," Ammu said with a sigh, like she was remembering when she and Khalamoni were kids.

"It hasn't changed much since the last time we were here. I expected it to," said Khalamoni.

"Come on, let's go up!" Mama said. He had two of the largest suitcases with him. He let Nadia,

Adam, Ammu, and Khalamoni go first on the elevator. The elevator took them up to the second floor. Somehow, Ammu and Khalamoni knew exactly where to go even though they hadn't been back here in years! Nadia wondered if she would remember exactly where everything was in her own house even after that long.

The door opened before they had the chance to ring the bell. In the doorway was . . . Nadia's nanu! It was the very first time Nadia had seen her nanu in person.

"Nadia, Adam!" Nanu said, her eyes landing on them before even Ammu and Khalamoni. She leaned forward and pulled them into an embrace. It was just the right amount of warm and smelled just like Nadia expected a nanu should—sweet mixed in with the smell of spices from the kitchen. Nadia loved it!

"Oh, you two have gotten so big!" Nanu said once she had let both of them go. She took them in with her warm brown eyes, and Nadia couldn't help but smile. She and Adam had seen their nanu on their phone screen many times. Nadia loved telling her nanu all about school, journalism, and Yasmin. But it was different seeing her in person. For one, she could see a lot more of her. On the phone, Nanu was usually a little too close to the phone screen.

"Ahem." Khalamoni cleared her throat loudly, playfully annoyed to have been left out of all the hugging.

"I haven't forgotten you two," Nanu said, standing up straight and extending her arms for a hug. Ammu and Khalamoni walked into them, their eyes closed. Nadia watched the smile on Ammu's face. Even though she had been annoyed before about spending the summer in Bangladesh, she kind of understood why it was important. She had never seen Ammu smile like that before. She must have missed her mom, just like Nadia would miss Ammu if she had to spend time away from her.

Nanu ushered them all inside, where Mami was

waiting for them with ice-cold lemonade. She had long, black hair, a round face, and a kind smile.

"You all must be so tired!" she said, handing everyone a glass. Nadia had never met her mami before either, though sometimes Ammu would give Nadia the phone when she was speaking to Mami. This was usually during birthdays or Eids, and Mami would say happy birthday or Eid Mubarak and that was that.

Now, Nadia took the glass of lemonade from her and drank it down in one big gulp. Refreshing!

Ammu and Khalamoni hugged Mami too, before sipping their lemonade and filling everyone in on the long plane journey. Sleep was still heavy on Nadia's eyelids, though, because she let out a big yawn. Probably the biggest yawn ever.

Everyone turned to look at her. Nadia flushed. She remembered it wasn't very polite to yawn when around other people.

"Let's get you all to sleep. We can catch up after," Nanu said before Nadia could say sorry for the impolite yawning. "Look at the two of them; they need their rest."

Everyone blinked at Nadia and Adam with sympathetic expressions. Nadia wanted to say that she was fine, but really she could use some sleep, even if it was daytime outside. So she didn't say much at all as Nanu hurried them into a small bedroom.

The last thought Nadia had as she lay down to sleep was . . . she couldn't believe she had to share a room with Adam of all people!

When Nadia woke up, she was confused. She glanced around the room and realized she was somewhere completely alien! The walls were salmon pink, and she was in a double bed beside Adam. Nadia hadn't shared a room (or a bed) with Adam since she was a baby.

She glanced up and heard the sound of laughter coming from outside the bedroom door. Some familiar voices—Ammu and Abbu, even Khalamoni—and some less familiar ones. It was then that Nadia remembered: She was in Bangladesh. In her family's home region of Sylhet.

It felt strange to be here, Nadia realized. Like home, but not really home at all. It had all of these things that felt familiar to Nadia, like the hand-woven Bangladeshi blanket Nadia and Adam were sleeping with. Nadia's family had one just like it at home. But then there were other things that were totally unfamiliar to Nadia. Like the slightly rusted steel wardrobe in a corner of the room, or the fact that the bed was harder than the one Nadia slept in at home.

"Do you think they're in there?" Nadia heard a whisper outside the door.

"Shh, you'll wake them up and we'll get in trouble," said another voice.

"You're being louder than I am!" the first voice said.

"I can hear you!" Nadia called, hoping the whispering would stop. There was silence for a moment and then the door clicked open. Two girls stood in the doorway. They had very round faces, and they wore the same blue and white outfit.

"Hello!" one of the girls said. They looked the exact same so it was difficult for Nadia to tell them apart. They were her cousins—her mama's twin daughters. Nadia had only spoken to them a few times on the phone, and that was just to say hello, or Eid Mubarak, before the phone was handed to someone else. Nadia had wondered what her cousins were really like.

"Hi," said Nadia, suddenly feeling shy. Her cousins were nine and a half years old—only one and a half years older than Nadia! But they looked so tall standing in front of her, and in the dim light, they even looked a little scary. Nadia didn't know what to say to them. She wished Adam would wake up so she wasn't all on her own meeting her cousins.

As if Adam had heard her silent wish, he twisted in bed and almost hit Nadia with an outstretched hand. Nadia jumped out of the way just at the last second.

She exchanged a glance with her two cousins, and a moment later the three of them burst out laughing. Like they were all in on an inside joke. Adam sat up, suddenly awake.

"What's going on?" he asked, rubbing his eyes. He squinted at his cousins. "Who are you?"

"I'm Lily," said the girl on the right.

"And I'm Rosie," said the one on the left.

"I'm Nadia," said Nadia.

"And I'm Adam," Adam grumbled rudely.

"Why are you wearing the same outfit?" Nadia asked.

Lily and Rosie looked down at their clothes, like they'd forgotten what they were wearing.

"Oh, it was our last day of school. This is our school uniform," Lily said.

"I like it," said Nadia. "We don't have school uniforms like this back at home."

"It's like a salwar kameez," Rosie added. Nadia could see that. It was a long blue and white top with matching trousers at the bottom. A lot like a salwar kameez.

"Did you have a nice sleep?" Lily asked after a moment. "Abbu said you two were very tired after your flight."

"It was a really long flight. Like . . . probably the longest flight ever," Nadia said. She wondered if Lily and Rosie had ever been on a flight as long as that.

"Hmm," Lily said. The two of them exchanged a glance that said they didn't quite believe that. "Come on out when you're ready. We're about to have dinner."

Nadia's stomach rumbled hungrily. She hadn't eaten since their flight from Dubai, and that felt like hours and hours ago. Sunlight was streaming in through the windows now, and it had been dark when their flight had landed.

"See you soon!" Lily and Rosie smiled, their dimples on display, as they hurried out the bedroom door.

A Delicious Welcome-Home Feast

Nadia climbed out of bed and looked at the bedroom around them. It was a little bigger than her bedroom at home. There was the big double bed where she and Adam had been sleeping and a desk with a computer. There was even a door to the side that led outside to a small balcony! Nadia's house back home didn't have any balconies at all, though Khalamoni's apartment did. Sometimes, when they visited Khalamoni in the summer, she would make iced tea and the two of them would sit outside on her balcony, drinking their iced teas and sharing stories. Nadia hoped she and Khalamoni could do that here as well.

Adam climbed out of bed too, stretching his

arms above his head and letting out a big yawn.

"Lily and Rosie were nice," Adam said. "Even if they *did* wake me up."

"Hmm," Nadia said. Lily and Rosie did seem nice, but she still wasn't sure how she was supposed to act around them. She had never met any of her cousins before, and Lily and Rosie seemed so much older than she was, and cooler too.

Nadia and Adam stepped outside of the bedroom and into the dining area. The dining table was already full of different kinds of dishes. Nadia could smell spicy biryani, creamy vegetable korma, and chicken bhuna. Her stomach grumbled even more loudly at the smell of all the delicious food.

"Nadia, Adam, you're awake!" Ammu said. She had changed into a pink-and-white salwar kameez, and her hair was damp like she had just stepped out of the shower. Nadia wanted to shower too. Her skin prickled with the summer heat.

"Shower first or dinner first?" Ammu asked, like she could read Nadia's mind.

"Dinner!" Nadia said at the same time Adam said, "Shower!"

"Uh-oh," said Abbu, like he could already sense an argument about to happen.

"Dinner will be nicer if we're all cleaned up first!" Adam said.

"But I'm hungry now!" complained Nadia. She had only eaten a little on the plane because the airplane food was *not* nice.

"I'm the oldest, so my opinion matters most!" declared Adam, like he often did.

"That's not fair!" replied Nadia, like *she* often did.

"Come on, you two. No fighting," Ammu said with a sigh.

"I'm the oldest in the whole family," Nanu said, stepping between Nadia and Adam. "And I say . . . we get cleaned up before dinner."

Nadia groaned, but she couldn't argue with Nanu.

After everybody was all cleaned up, and Nadia was hungrier than ever, the whole family sat around the dinner table. There were too many of them to really fit, but they managed to squeeze into all the corner spaces until the table was so full that Nadia was elbow to elbow with Adam.

She felt a little shy, but she didn't mind it so much when Nanu piled biryani, vegetable korma, and chicken bhuna onto her plate. She mixed up the rice of the biryani with the korma and chicken bhuna before taking a bite with her hands. Delicious! Back home, Nadia sometimes ate with a knife and fork because Ammu and Abbu said she had to practice how to use her cutlery. But she much preferred eating with her hands. It made the food taste even better. And Nanu's food was already so amazing.

"Mmm," Nadia said, and Nanu smiled at her appreciatively.

"Are you sure the three of you will be okay doing Ramadan this year? It's been a long time since you've fasted in Bangladesh. The heat can be a lot to handle," Nanu said. Nadia was surprised she was saying this to her ammu, abbu, and khalamoni. They were adults and had been fasting their

whole lives! Did Nanu really think they wouldn't be able to fast in the heat?

"We'll be fine, Amma," Ammu said, waving Nanu's concerns away like it was nothing. "It's not so easy to fast back home either, you know. It gets hot there too."

"Not like here," Nanu said, almost like she was proud of the heat here.

"I'm going to fast this year too!" Nadia chimed in. Everybody turned to look at her again, with concern all over their faces. Nadia hadn't said anything rude this time, had she?

"Are you sure, Nadia?" Ammu asked slowly, like she was carefully picking her words. "It's going to be hard, and you've never fasted before."

Nadia was confused. Ammu and Abbu had told both her and Adam that they could start fasting when they were eight years old, and now finally Nadia was old enough. It wouldn't be the same without Yasmin by her side, but she still wanted to do it.

"I'm sure!" Nadia said. "I told you I was going to fast this year. Yasmin and I made a plan."

"Yes, but that was before we decided to come to Bangladesh. And Yasmin isn't here to help you through it. It would be okay if you wanted to wait until next year, and then you and Yasmin could still have your plan to help each other through Ramadan," Ammu said.

Nadia shook her head. She couldn't just give up because their plans had changed. She and Yasmin had already decided.

"We're going to video chat," Nadia said, making it sound like it was the same thing as seeing each other in person even though she knew it wasn't.

"It's not going to be easy, Nadia," Abbu said cautiously.

"I can do it!" Nadia exclaimed. Lily and Rosie exchanged a glance Nadia didn't understand, and Adam rolled his eyes like Nadia was being silly. But she could do it, she knew that for sure. After all, Adam had been allowed to fast last year. He had kept a whole of ten fasts, and he had said it wasn't difficult at all. Nadia knew he had at least a little bit of trouble because there had been one afternoon when she came home from school to find Adam lying on the couch, asleep, still in his school clothes! He had to have been tired for that.

"Weren't we even younger than Nadia when we started fasting?" Khalamoni asked. She gave Nadia a supportive grin. Nadia knew she could always count on Khalamoni.

"I was eight," Ammu said, with a faraway look in her eyes like she was remembering the time when she was eight.

"And you tried to fast when you were just six years old because you wanted to keep up with your sister," Nanu said to Khalamoni with a fond grin. Everyone burst into giggles at the idea. Even Khalamoni, though she looked a little cross at being exposed by Nanu.

"Well, gone are those days," Ammu said. "Now, it's a wonder any of us can keep up with her when she's always so busy with her journalist job.

Running around to different cities and countries."

"Hey, I barely ever leave the country!" Khalamoni said defensively. "And I only pitched this article as an excuse to come back home." At this, Khalamoni gave Nadia a conspiratorial wink, like only Nadia knew that coming back to Bangladesh was an excuse for her work and not the other way around.

"What's your story about anyway? You haven't shared much," Mama said as he scooped another helping of biryani onto his plate and even loaded some onto Nadia's plate. Nadia didn't mind. This was the best biryani she'd ever had, and she was sure she could eat at least two more platefuls of it.

"I'm researching the rising sea levels. The ongoing floods. The people displaced," Khalamoni said.

Suddenly, it was like all the air had been sucked out of the room. Nadia looked around, trying to understand why the tone of the conversation had suddenly changed. Where everybody had been laughing and joking just a few moments ago, now everyone had grim faces. Even Ammu and Abbu. Nadia wanted to ask what was going on, but she was afraid of suddenly saying the wrong thing.

"It's awful, isn't it?" Mami asked with a sigh. "We know so many people who have been affected by the most recent floods."

Mama nodded too and reached out a hand to rest it on Mami's shoulder.

Nadia had never been so confused.

"What floods?" Nadia asked. She couldn't enjoy her big feast in peace if she didn't know what was going on! She had seen news reports on flooding in some of the towns and cities around where they lived. But usually, the flooding would stop after a day or two, and then things would go back to normal. She didn't know why everyone would be so grim about the topic of floods!

Khalamoni looked at Ammu, like she was asking permission to tell Nadia. Nadia couldn't help but feel annoyed. She wasn't a baby anymore—she was a journalist who could understand real-life things! She wished her family would realize that.

"Well, in Bangladesh there are floods almost every year," Khalamoni said. "And they seem to get worse and worse every year as well."

"But don't floods just last for a few days?" Nadia asked.

"No, Nadia. Floods here can last a long time, and they destroy a lot," Khalamoni explained. "People's houses, cars, roads . . . and they can ruin farms and crops too."

"I didn't see anything like that here!" Nadia said. In fact, it had been sunny since she got to Bangladesh, and she hadn't seen any floods at all.

"Our area hasn't been hit too hard during the floods this year," Nanu said. "But a lot of people in Sylhet have been. Even some of our family members."

Mami nodded sadly. "One of my uncles lost everything. They had a farm just outside the city, and the floods ruined their crops and destroyed their home. Your mama and I helped their family move in with some relatives we have in Dhaka. But . . . they still don't know how they'll rebuild everything they've lost."

Nadia didn't know what to say. She was pretty sure when she learned about floods in school it was about places she had never been to and people she would never know. She had no idea that floods could affect the city her parents were from and even people her family knew. It was a little strange to think about and made Nadia feel sad in the pit of her stomach. She didn't like that feeling at all.

Nadia wanted to ask more questions, but the conversation had moved on. Abbu was talking about his work in an insurance company, and Ammu was telling Nanu about how Nadia had gotten excellent grades in English that year. It was like nobody wanted to talk about the floods for too long. But Nadia still had so many questions. She made a mental note to ask Khalamoni her questions later. After all, she was the one writing about it. Nadia was sure all her questions would be answered soon.

A Family Game Night!

After dinner, Nadia and her entire family went into the sitting room. Nadia thought maybe they'd watch TV together. In Yasmin's house sometimes after dinner, her parents would put on a fun movie to watch and relax.

But Mama didn't turn on the TV. Instead, he took out boxes of board games from the shelf underneath the coffee table.

"Let's see . . ." he said, setting the games down on the table in front of him. "We have Monopoly, ludo, Snakes and Ladders. . . ." He started listing off each of the games.

"Here's something you can put in your notebook, Nadia," Khalamoni said. "Did you know that ludo and Snakes and Ladders were both invented in South Asia?"

Nadia hadn't known that. She quickly scribbled it down into her notebook. Ms. Johnson and Mr. McGrane might be very impressed by her knowledge of South Asian board games.

"I haven't played ludo since the last time we were all together," Ammu said.

"There are a few too many of us to play here, though," Mama said, looking all around.

"Let's play Monopoly," Khalamoni said, picking up the box. "I've never seen a Bangladeshi version

of it before." Nadia looked at the box as well. All the names of places were in Bangla, which Nadia couldn't read.

"We can write down all the names in English in Post-it notes so everyone can play," Ammu suggested.

So it was settled. Mama opened up the box, and they moved the coffee table so everyone could sit on the floor to play. Lily and Rosie decided to play as one team, and Nadia asked Khalamoni if they could be on a team together. They were always the best team.

Then, they all sat down to play the game. Nadia had never played such an intense game of Monopoly before, and Mama's family had their own rules different from Ammu and Abbu's rules. Like when Nadia played at home, they were never allowed to do trades with other players, but according to Mama any and all trades were allowed.

Which was a good thing because Nadia and

Khalamoni tricked Ammu into a trade for all of the railway stations.

Khalamoni high-fived Nadia. "We're definitely going to win this!"

Ammu frowned. "I don't like these rules. It feels like cheating."

Mama shrugged his shoulders. "This is how the real world works, you know."

Nadia giggled. She couldn't believe Ammu and her siblings were being just as competitive as Nadia and Adam.

The game went on for ages. Finally, Adam and Ammu were both bankrupt, and Nanu was too tired to play.

"I think we should win by default. We have the most money and the most assets," Khalamoni argued.

"Fine, but this isn't over," Mama said. "Next week, I'll beat you in ludo."

"We'll see," Khalamoni said with a smile.

A Ramadan Challenge Is Issued!

"I can't believe you've never kept a fast for Ramadan before!" Lily said the next day as the four of them sat on the swings on the playground outside Mama's apartment. Nadia was beginning to recognize the differences between her twin cousins, even though they looked identical. When they smiled, Rosie had dimples on both cheeks, while Lily only had a dimple on her right cheek. Lily had a slightly higher voice when she spoke, and Rosie had a slightly rounder face. They both dressed in colorful outfits, but Rosie preferred to wear more reds, pinks, and greens while Lily wore more yellows, oranges, and blues.

"It's because Nadia is a baby, so Ammu and

Abbu wouldn't let her fast until she was more grown up," Adam said, as if he had been fasting his whole life and wasn't just a year older than Nadia.

"I'm not a baby," Nadia huffed. She couldn't believe Adam was teaming up with their cousins against her. "Ammu and Abbu only allow us to start fasting when we're eight years old. Adam didn't even start fasting until last year!"

But Nadia's cousins didn't seem very impressed by her explanations.

"We started fasting when we were seven years old," Rosie said. "Because *our* parents thought we were mature enough to start fasting really early."

Nadia felt her stomach drop. Seven? And now Lily and Rosie were nine and a half years old, which meant they'd been fasting for three years! They had so much experience, and Nadia had none.

"Well, it doesn't matter," Nadia said, trying to sound like she didn't care even though it felt like it mattered a lot. "I'll fast this year, and it'll be great!"

"How many fasts are you going to keep?" Rosie asked. She was only a little taller than Nadia, but from the way she looked at Nadia, it felt like she towered over her. Nadia felt heat rise to her cheeks.

"I'm going to keep . . ." She thought about how many Adam had kept last year. "Seven."

Lily and Rosie exchanged a glance before bursting into giggles. They didn't sound like friendly giggles, and Nadia didn't join in.

"Seven? You *are* a baby," Lily said. "Rosie and I kept ten fasts last year."

"I almost kept eleven, but my ammu insisted I break the last one." Rosie shrugged.

"I can keep eleven fasts this year," Nadia said, even though she wasn't quite sure. She knew fasting was difficult, and Yasmin and she had promised each other they would take it slow since it was their first year fasting.

"I can keep eleven fasts too. Probably twelve,"

Adam said, looking at Nadia with a smug smile.

"Well, we're going to try and keep even more this year," Rosie said.

"We're almost adults now, and adults have to keep all twenty-nine . . . or thirty," Lily said.

They wouldn't find out exactly how many fasts to keep until Ramadan was almost over, and they tried to see if there was a new moon in the sky. The new moon meant Eid would be the next day—so twenty-nine days of fasting. No new moon meant Eid would be two days later—so thirty days of fasting.

"I'm almost an adult too," Adam said, even though he was only a year older than Nadia. And Nadia was pretty sure her cousins were only a few months older than Adam. Could they really keep all the fasts this year?

Nadia tried to bite down her fear as she sat up straight and declared, "I'll keep just as many fasts as the rest of you."

"Psh," Lily scoffed, like Nadia had said something

completely unbelievable. But Nadia had never been one to back down from a challenge, and she didn't like losing. Back home, Nadia and Adam had races for everything. Like a race to see who could finish setting the table first, or who could finish all their homework before the other. It even made chores fun sometimes. And Nadia almost *always* won.

"I can do it," Nadia insisted.

"Okay, let's see then who can keep the most fasts this Ramadan," Rosie said, looking at each of them in turn. "I'm the oldest, so I say it'll be me."

"You're only older than me by like ten minutes," Lily said, rolling her eyes.

"I'm going to keep the most fasts," Adam insisted.

"If it's a proper challenge, there'll have to be a winner," Rosie said. They had forgotten all about playing together on the playground filled with slides, swings, and a seesaw, now that a new game was on the horizon. "And the winner gets . . ."

"Everyone's Eidi on Eid day!" Lily chimed in.

Nadia's eyes widened. Eidi was money that adults gave to kids on Eid day. Usually, Nadia and Adam got Eidi from their parents and aunties and uncles from the Bengali community. They usually pooled their money together to buy candy and soda from the shop so they could have a small Eid feast just for the two of them. It was one of the things that made Eid feel special.

But taking everyone's Eidi on Eid day didn't sound special. Nadia hoped that Adam or Rosie would say something. But when she looked around, both of them were nodding in agreement.

"And . . . the person who keeps the *least* amount of fasts won't be allowed to go out to play or to the shops on Eid day," Rosie added. "Because they're obviously the baby who couldn't handle Ramadan, so they don't get to have fun on Eid."

Nadia's stomach churned at the thought of an Eid without playing with her brother or treating themselves to their favorite candies. If she lost, it meant she would have to spend Eid with the boring adults while her brother and cousins had their own fun.

None of it sounded like the spirit of Eid. To Nadia, Eid was all about spending time with family and friends, going to the mosque, and eating really good food. But she couldn't disagree with her older cousins. She nodded in agreement too.

Now, Nadia just had to beat everyone and keep the most fasts.

A Climate Disaster!

The next day, Nadia woke up bright and early, before even Adam or her cousins, and headed outside the bedroom. Khalamoni was at the dinner table, chewing on a piece of porota while reading a Bengali newspaper.

"What are you reading?" Nadia asked, hopping onto the seat next to Khalamoni and pulling a porota and dim bhaji onto her own breakfast plate. She had her sparkly purple notebook with her, ready to write down all the things she had been learning since she arrived in Bangladesh.

"It's just a Bangladeshi newspaper," Khalamoni said, folding up the paper and putting it down on the table in front of her. Still, Nadia could see the front page. The headline said: "Monsoon Season Could Mean Further Climate Disaster."

Nadia was confused. She had learned about climate change in school. The field trip to the science museum meant she knew all about renewable energy, water conservation, and even the ozone layer. But she didn't know how that was related to the newspaper headline here.

"What's monsoon?" Nadia asked.

Khalamoni looked thoughtful for a moment before replying, "Monsoon is one of the seasons in Bangladesh. In Bangla we call it borsha."

Nadia nodded. She'd heard that word being used before. "Why are people worried about it?"

"Borsha, or monsoon, is the season of rain. It's the season when Bangladesh gets a lot of heavy rainfall. It's when flooding is the most likely to happen. If it rains a lot, the rivers overflow and the cities and villages flood," Khalamoni said. "Monsoon has already started, and so many places have flooded. People are worried that the floods will just get worse and worse during the season."

Even though Nadia knew what flooding was, she was having a hard time imagining the kind of flooding that Khalamoni was describing. She definitely didn't like the idea of cities and villages being filled up with floodwater! Where would the people in the villages and cities go?

"Can't we do something before it gets worse?" Nadia asked.

"It's a difficult situation," Khalamoni said. "That's one of the things that's a struggle here. The land in Bangladesh is very low-lying, which is why we have so many floods here. And with sea levels rising globally, it means slowly we're losing land to the sea. The long-term solution is to figure out a way to stop our land from going underwater, which will hopefully also stop all of this flooding. The Netherlands had a similar problem as Bangladesh's; they built structures that protect the country from flooding, like dams. So there are solutions, but it's only really the government that can do something long-term, and only with a lot of money and support."

Khalamoni paused before shaking her head, giving Nadia a smile. "You don't worry too much about it, Nadia. I have to keep up with all of this because that's what my story is about, so I have to do the research, and create the links between the recent floods and long-term effects of climate change, and figure out how people are dealing with it all here."

"But I *want* to worry about it!" Nadia exclaimed. Before speaking to her khalamoni, she hadn't even known that Bangladesh was in any kind of danger, even though they'd learned about climate change in school. Nadia wanted to learn even more, and she wanted to help.

"I know you need ideas for the school newspaper, but you can focus on the positive things about Bangladesh. A lot of the times when people write about countries like Bangladesh, they only focus on the negatives, but it's important to talk about the positives too. Like the things you learn and all the fun you're going to have this summer," Khalamoni said with a definitive nod.

Nadia knew she could, but she felt like everything she was learning about climate change and Bangladesh was even more important. Even if she didn't write about it for her school newspaper, she wanted to know more!

"But . . . I want to help you with your research. I want to be a real journalist. Please?" Nadia asked.

"Okay, maybe you can come along with me when I interview the Talukdar family," Khalamoni said thoughtfully. "But you have to be very professional when we go and visit them. It's an official interview."

Nadia smiled, pleased that Khalamoni was finally seeing her as someone who could be helpful and not just as a kid spending her summer vacation in Bangladesh.

"Can I come up with some interview questions to ask too? I've been practicing coming up with serious interrogative ones!" Nadia said. She pulled out her notebook and showed Khalamoni the questions she had written down about Bangladesh. She'd already gotten answers for some of them without even asking anybody.

Khalamoni nodded at what Nadia had written, though she seemed distracted. "Sure, yes. You can come up with some questions."

Nadia wanted to know if she could also ask the Talukdar family her questions and really interview them, but she wasn't sure if Khalamoni would think that was "professional," and she was worried that she would change her mind. She didn't want Khalamoni to think she was too much of a baby to help out.

"When's the interview?" she asked instead. She had to make sure she was prepared.

"They actually just got back to me to schedule a date. Let me see . . ." Khalamoni mumbled as she opened up her phone and clicked on her calendar. She scrolled down a list of things marked in different colors. Nadia had no idea that Khalamoni was such a busy person. "This week, they're in Dhaka, so . . . it'll be in two weeks' time." Khalamoni's eyebrows wrinkled up, like the date was confusing for her. "That'll be the second day of Ramadan, and it's in the afternoon, so it'll be only a few hours before iftar time. Do you think you can do that, Nadia? It won't be too much?"

Nadia wasn't sure. If she wasn't doing the Ramadan race, she could just not fast on that day. But now she didn't really have a choice. If she didn't fast, she'd fall behind and lose the competition. Then her cousins and brother would never take her seriously and would always think of her as a baby. And maybe even Khalamoni wouldn't be able to see that she could be a journalist and help her with her climate change article.

Nadia was tired of being seen as a baby. She was ready to be a grown-up.

So, she nodded her head as confidently as she could.

"I can do it, for sure!" she said, even though she wasn't so sure at all.

Nadia and Yasmin Are Not on the Same Page

The days in Bangladesh were so different from the ones back home. At home, Nadia would be spending her summer vacation playing video games with Adam or hanging out with Yasmin. Maybe they would go to the park or visit the mall with their moms. But in Bangladesh, Nadia and Adam spent their time hanging out with their cousins. They played board games, like ludo or Snakes and Ladders together. Once Lily and Rosie got a big board out of their bedroom, and they played a game called Carrom Board. Nadia had never heard of that game before. Other times, they played racing games on Lily and Rosie's gaming console, or outside in the playground.

Sometimes, Ammu and Abbu would take the whole family out to travel. They visited family members Nadia had never met before or went to restaurants to have delicious food. Once, Ammu decided they would eat at a street food cart. They ate spicy fuchka on the side of the road. Nadia loved the hard flour shell and the spicy chickpea filling inside, but Ammu told her she could only have one plate.

But sometimes, Nadia didn't go outside at all because it was too hot. She could only lie in bed, under a fan, wishing that it would cool down. She wasn't used to the heat or the humidity. She didn't like how the heat made her sweat so much, and how she had to take multiple showers in a single day. There were times when Lily and Rosie wanted to play outside, but Nadia stayed indoors. On those days, Nanu always cut up delicious Bangladeshi fruits that Nadia had never tried before: sweet mangoes and guavas, sour amras, and slippery kathal.

All throughout, Nadia was counting down to Ramadan in her head. Her very first day of fasting was soon approaching. When Ramadan was only two days away, Nadia decided to video chat Yasmin. The two of them had been texting back and forth all summer, but they hadn't had the chance for a video chat yet. Nadia missed hanging out with her best friend. Ammu told her that she had to wait until it wasn't too late at night or early morning back home, so it was after dinner that she finally made the call.

Yasmin answered on her tablet quickly, and her familiar face on Nadia's screen filled her up with warmth. She almost felt like she was back home, watching movies and eating popcorn with Yasmin.

"Yasmin!" Nadia said.

"Nadia!" said Yasmin, her face breaking out into a grin. Yasmin was just the same, with her dark-brown skin and her black hair in twists and tied up with colorful ball bobbles.

"What are you doing?" Nadia asked. She could hear the sound of clinking behind Yasmin, and Yasmin's mom speaking loudly into the phone.

"Preparing for Ramadan. It's starting so soon and my mom is freaking out!" Yasmin said. "She bought so much stuff, and she even said she was going to make all my favorite foods for our first iftar."

Some of Nadia's happiness faded away. She wished that she was right beside Yasmin on that first iftar, eating all her favorite foods. Last

Ramadan, Yasmin's parents had come to break fast with Nadia's family. They'd brought over plantains, jollof rice, and moin moin. Nadia sometimes ate Nigerian food when she visited Yasmin, but it was extra special to have Yasmin's whole family share the foods they usually ate during Ramadan with Nadia's whole family. Nadia wished she could have them again, with Yasmin by her side. That would make it even more special.

"It's sad we're not spending Ramadan together," Nadia said finally.

"I'm sad about it too," Yasmin said. "But . . . you're having a good time in Bangladesh, right?"

Nadia shrugged. "I guess. It's fun to hang out with my cousins and meet my family, even though it's really hot so I get tired sometimes."

"What are your cousins like?" Yasmin asked. Her cousins lived in other cities in America, and sometimes during the weekends or holidays, she and her family would drive out to visit them. But this was Nadia's first time meeting cousins.

"They're older than me, and they have a lot of opinions," Nadia said. She didn't want to admit that it was a little scary to be the youngest kid in the house. "They even came up with this idea to do a Ramadan race. I'm excited for that. I'm going to win!"

"A Ramadan race?" Yasmin drew her eyebrows together in confusion.

"We're going to try and see who can keep the most fasts this Ramadan. My cousins, Lily and Rosie, think they'll win because they're the oldest. And Adam thinks he'll win because he's Adam." Nadia rolled her eyes at that. "But I'm pretty sure I can win and nobody will even see it coming."

Yasmin didn't seem as excited as Nadia felt. "Are you sure a Ramadan race is a good idea? It sounds . . . difficult."

"But I can do it; I can win!" Nadia said. She didn't know why Yasmin wasn't being more supportive, but maybe she also thought Nadia couldn't win. She had hoped Yasmin would understand.

"Okay . . ." Yasmin said, though she didn't sound very impressed. "Well, what about your article for the school newspaper? How's that going? Do you have ideas?"

Nadia brightened. At least Yasmin was excited about that. "It's going okay. I'm writing down all of the things I'm learning. Like the super-long flight over here, and how there are eight regions in Bangladesh, and how people here sometimes play this game called Carrom Board. But . . . I really want to help Khalamoni with the article she's writing. Maybe it will give me ideas for my article too."

"What's she writing about?" Yasmin asked, leaning forward like she really wanted to hold on to every word Nadia was saying. It made Nadia feel even more excited.

"Well, it's about climate change. And floods. Khalamoni said there are floods in Bangladesh and there are a lot of people who are affected by them. We're going to interview someone together soon. I can't wait! My first real-life interview!"

Yasmin's eyes widened. "Wow, that's so cool! I bet Ms. Johnson would love it if you wrote about that."

"Maybe," Nadia said. Ms. Johnson was definitely interested in climate change, but their last project had been all about that. Wouldn't Ms. Johnson be more interested in something she knew nothing about? Something that was new and exciting!

"I mean, I didn't even have any idea about floods in Bangladesh. I bet Ms. Johnson doesn't either. So you'll really be a real-life journalist. Writing about something to make everyone in our school aware," Yasmin said.

Yasmin wasn't wrong. They hadn't learned anything about Bangladesh from the science museum or their climate change projects, even though Yasmin and Nadia's project had been all about water.

"Khalamoni told me that she was writing a feature about climate change, so she'll interview a lot of people and even give her own opinion. If I write a feature about Bangladesh, maybe I could write about the Ramadan race, and about climate change too," Nadia said thoughtfully.

"Maybe I can help you," Yasmin said. "I could . . . draw some pictures of the things you write about? Then when it's on the front page, they could use my drawing alongside it, and that could be my submission for the school newspaper."

Nadia loved that idea. Yasmin was an amazing artist. For Nadia's birthday last year, Yasmin drew her a birthday card as a comic strip where Nadia was a journalist traveling all over the world and reporting on everything going on. In one panel, Journalist Nadia was interviewing a cat that was stuck in a tree! In another, Nadia was reviewing a five-star restaurant and their amazing food. It was one of Nadia's prized possessions and she kept the birthday card on her bedside table.

She definitely wanted Yasmin's artistic talents to help her article, and maybe Nadia's journalistic talents would help make Yasmin's artwork shine too. They were the perfect team.

"Yes!" Nadia exclaimed. "I can tell you all about what I learn here and you can draw something that captures everything."

"And it'll feel like I was in Bangladesh, right by your side all summer!"

Or at least as close to that as they could get when Yasmin wasn't actually in Bangladesh, Nadia thought.

"When is the interview?" Yasmin asked.

"The second day of Ramadan," Nadia admitted. "And I've been trying to come up with interview questions, but it's hard. I wonder how Millie Davies comes up with good interview questions."

"Hmm," Yasmin said. "Maybe you can pretend to interview *me*, and that will give you ideas for questions."

Nadia liked that idea. She sat up in her chair and put on a serious expression.

"What is your opinion about climate change?" Nadia asked the first question that came into her head.

"It's definitely very bad," Yasmin said, before bursting into a fit of giggles. Nadia couldn't help but join in, even though that's definitely *not* how a real journalist would behave.

"I don't think that was a very good question," Nadia said when they had both stopped laughing. "I already know climate change is bad."

"Maybe you could ask *why* it's bad, or why it's happening in Bangladesh," Yasmin said.

"Hmm . . ." Nadia said, quickly scribbling down those questions in her notebook. She still didn't feel like they were the kind of questions that would make her editor in chief, but at least it was a start.

NADIA ISLAM'S FACTS ABOUT BANGLADESH

#1: Bangladesh became a country in the year
1971. That's three years *after* Nanu was born!

#2: Bangladesh has eight different regions:
Barishal, Chittagong, Dhaka, Khulna, Rajshahi,
Rangpur, Mymensingh, and Sylhet. My entire
family is from Sylhet!

#3: Bangladesh's national animal is the royal
Bengal tiger—they live in the Sundarbans forest.
(That's nowhere near Sylhet.)

#4: Bangladesh loves tea! The adults in the house
drink tea all the time and every guest who
comes over is served tea too. There are lots
of tea gardens in Sylhet. They're beautiful and
green. And Sylhet has a famous kind of tea
called the seven-layer tea!

#5: Bangladesh has a lot of amazing celebrations!
Khalamoni's favorite is Boi Mela, a book festival
that lasts all of February. Nanu likes Bijoy
Dibosh, Victory Day. Ammu and Abbu love
Pohela Boishakh, which is the Bengali new year.

CHAPTER 11

The Islam Family Prepares for Ramadan

When Nadia's family started preparing for Ramadan, she felt like maybe Bangladesh wasn't so different from home after all. Mami had already started shopping for Eid outfits. She showed Nadia some of the websites where she usually bought Eid clothes. Mama made a du'a booklet for everyone in the family. It had all of the prayers that were important to remember during Ramadan in Arabic, Bengali, and English! He told Nadia that every year he even made copies of his handmade prayer booklet to give to the local mosque. Mama worked as a graphic designer, so he knew all about how to design the du'a booklet so it looked like a real book when printed out!

Nadia couldn't wait for Ramadan to start, even if she still missed Yasmin. At least she was going to spend Ramadan challenging her cousins and Adam. And she was already becoming a better journalist, thanks to Khalamoni. Once Khalamoni's interviews began, she would be sure to learn even more.

During dinner a few days before Ramadan started, Nanu asked everyone the same question that Ammu always did the week before Ramadan: What were the family's goals during Ramadan?

Ammu said she wanted to read the Qur'an from start to finish. That was *always* her goal for Ramadan. Mama and Abbu wanted to go to the mosque for Taraweeh as often as they could. Taraweeh was a special prayer that you carried out during the month of Ramadan. Mami and Khalamoni wanted to learn some new surahs from the Qur'an.

When Nanu asked Rosie what she wanted to do for Ramadan, Nadia wondered if her cousin would talk about the Ramadan race.

"I just want to keep as many fasts as I can," Rosie said solemnly. But Nadia could see the mischievous glint in her eyes.

"Me too!" Lily agreed.

"But you have to pace yourselves," Mama said sternly. "Fasting is hard work, and it's okay if you can't keep as many as you want to. It's not fardh for you to fast yet." *Fardh* was an Arabic word that meant something was a must for Muslims. Like how the adults *had* to fast for all the days of Ramadan.

"I want to keep a lot of fasts too this year, more than I did last year!" Adam said excitedly. Nadia could tell from the looks he exchanged with Lily and Rosie that he was thinking about the Ramadan race.

"Nadia, what about you?" Nanu asked.

"I want to keep a lot of fasts too!" Nadia said determinedly. She looked at her cousins and her brother, so they knew that she wasn't going to back down from their challenge!

"Well, you should start off slow, Nadia," Ammu said to her. "It's your first year fasting. Maybe your goal should be to keep just a few fasts to ease you into Ramadan."

Nadia couldn't believe Ammu wanted her to have a different goal than Adam or Lily or Rosie. Nobody had told *them* to only try and keep a few fasts.

"But I can keep more than just a few!" Nadia insisted. "I can keep just as many as Adam, or Lily, or Rosie."

"Okay, but it's also all right if you don't want to keep as many fasts as them," Ammu said. "Lily and Rosie have already fasted before, and so has Adam, but it's your first time. It'll take you a little while to adjust to it. Don't put too much pressure on yourself, Nadia."

Then, the family moved on to what kind of shopping they would do to prepare for Ramadan, and the kinds of foods they wanted to eat each iftar. But Nadia just sat with her arms crossed, annoyed that everyone in her family saw her as a baby. She would have to show all of them that she was way more mature than they thought. She would find a way to keep more fasts than Adam, Lily, and Rosie.

As everyone prepared for Ramadan to start in just a few days, Nadia and Khalamoni had something else to worry about: the big interview!

Khalamoni had been researching every day, and even Nadia had tried to learn more about climate change in Bangladesh. She'd looked up news articles online but a lot of them were in Bengali (which she couldn't read), and even the ones in English were difficult for her to understand.

"What kind of interview questions are you going to ask?" Nadia asked Khalamoni one afternoon while they were out for a walk in a park near their house.

"Hmm, well . . . I already have a lot of information about the climate change situation in Bangladesh from my research, so I'll probably ask them specific questions about the kind of work that they've done," Khalamoni said.

Nadia wanted Khalamoni's help with coming up with her own questions, but she was already so busy! Nadia wished again that Yasmin was here. She would know just how to help Nadia. Yasmin always helped Nadia brainstorm, and Nadia helped Yasmin.

Now, Nadia had to figure things out on her own!

Before Nadia knew, it was already the first day of Ramadan. Ammu shook her awake for fajr. She blinked slowly, trying to rub sleep out of her eyes with balled-up fists.

"You don't have to fast today if you don't want to, Nadia," Ammu said. Nadia barely processed the words. She was still half asleep! But she could see the blurry shapes of her cousins and Adam in the background and hear the hum of their voices. That woke her up more than Ammu's attempts.

She jolted up in bed and tried to ignore that her

head still felt fuzzy with sleep.

"I'm ready!" She tried to say the words triumphantly, but they came out as little more than a mumble.

Ammu didn't look convinced. "Okay, well, fajr is soon, so wash your face and come to the breakfast table."

Nadia nodded before jumping out of bed and into the bathroom. She splashed water on her face, and that finally woke her up properly.

It was her first sehri! Excitement pulsed through her at the thought, even though she wasn't sure why she'd had to wake up so early.

When Nadia arrived at the breakfast table a few minutes later, everyone was already there. Nanu placed a bowl of rice on the table, alongside a bowl of vegetables and a plate of chicken.

Nadia didn't feel like eating any of those things! It was three in the morning. Way too early for Nadia to eat rice!

"I don't feel like eating," Nadia groaned.

"Nadia, if you don't eat, you won't be able to fast," Ammu said. She spooned some rice onto her plate and even put some on Nadia's plate.

"Why do I have to eat now? There's still time until dawn!" Nadia complained. She knew all about Ramadan, and how you were supposed to fast from sunrise to sunset. But it was still dark outside, so it definitely wasn't time for sunrise yet.

"We have to eat *before* dawn. Once it's time for fajr you won't be able to eat anymore. Fajr prayer is right before dawn, so it'll be too late if we wait until then," Abbu explained. "This way, we have plenty of time to eat instead of having to rush. Now eat up."

Nanu placed some vegetables and some chicken on her plate, right beside the rice Ammu had given her.

Nadia used her hands to mix the rice and chicken together, even though she still didn't feel like eating. She knew she wouldn't be allowed to fast if she didn't finish her food, and her cousins

114

were already halfway through their meal. Adam was half dozing, his eyes blinking awake every few minutes. And Lily and Rosie were leaning against each other as they ate, like they needed support to get through their early morning meal.

"What if I forget to wake up early? Does it mean I can't fast that day?" Nadia asked while chewing on her first bite of rice, chicken, and vegetables.

"Eating sehri isn't a *must*, but it definitely helps keep the hunger away," Abbu said with a smile.

"And you're going to need your energy to fast in the heat here," Khalamoni added.

"It's too early for so much talking!" Adam groaned through a mouthful of rice. "Just hurry up and eat before fajr prayer!"

Nadia stuck her tongue out at Adam, but he was right. Nadia had to finish her meal before time was up. She'd never eaten with a time limit before. Especially at such an odd time.

After sehri, clearing the table, and praying fajr, Nadia was too tired to function. She had never realized how tiring it must be to wake up early every day of Ramadan! She shuffled to the bedroom she and Adam were sharing. Adam was already fast asleep, but Nadia was full of food and water. She felt like her belly could burst.

Still, she crawled into bed and closed her eyes, and before she knew it, she was fast asleep.

NADIA ISLAM'S FACTS ABOUT RAMADAN

#1: Ramadan is one of the months in the Muslim calendar. It's the ninth month and it's a holy month. It's the month when Muslims fast! Being Muslim and Bangladeshi is amazing because it means we can have multiple new years. We have the Islamic calendar and the Islamic new year, the Bengali calendar and the Bengali new year, and the Gregorian calendar and its new year. That's three new years in just one year!

#2: The date for Ramadan is different every year! The Muslim calendar is based on the moon cycle and that's why it has no fixed dates. It's why nobody knows the date that Eid will be. Ammu says when they were kids, they would go out on the 29th day of Ramadan, looking everywhere for the new moon. If they spotted it, it meant the next day was Eid. If they didn't, it meant they had to fast one more day.

#3: During Ramadan, Muslims don't eat or drink anything from dawn until dusk (not even water)! At dawn, we eat a meal called sehri, and at dusk we eat a meal called iftar. If we don't eat those meals, we can still fast, but it's really difficult. Skipping those meals is not recommended!

#4: We love Ramadan, even if sometimes it's a little difficult to fast. So, during Ramadan you can greet Muslims by saying, "Ramadan Mubarak!"

#5: At the end of Ramadan, there's a celebration called Eid al-Fitr. We wear new clothes, pray a special Eid prayer, and we eat lots and lots of food!

CHAPTER 12

A Rousing Success for Nadia's First Day of Ramadan

Nadia didn't wake up again until noon. She blinked against the glaring sun, and for a moment she forgot that it was the first day of Ramadan.

But then she remembered waking up in the middle of the night to eat sehri, and it all dawned on her. She pulled out her purple notebook and wrote down all about her first time having sehri. She didn't want to forget. She knew it was a once-in-a-lifetime experience. She only wished Yasmin was here for her to talk to about it. But with the time difference, it was still the middle of the night for her.

Last Ramadan, Nadia remembered that she

woke first before everyone else because she hadn't woken up to eat sehri. This Ramadan, though, she could already hear the sound of her parents talking outside her bedroom door!

Adam, though, was still asleep, and when Nadia went outside looking for her cousins, Mama said they were still sleeping too. Nadia felt energized from the excitement of her first Ramadan, and she wanted to do something fun instead of sleeping all day!

"Are you feeling ready to come with me to the interview tomorrow?" Khalamoni asked her when Nadia walked over to her in the sitting room. She had her laptop open in front of her and looked hard at work.

Nadia had almost forgotten that the interview was tomorrow.

"Yes!" she said.

"Do you have your interview questions ready?" Khalamoni asked.

Nadia felt a flush of embarrassment.

"No," she admitted. "Millie Davies had the best interview questions for our teachers when she interviewed them for our school newspaper, but I know I can't ask those questions. And I tried to come up with my own, but I didn't know what makes good questions for an interview."

Khalamoni didn't look disappointed in Nadia. Instead, she put away her laptop and patted the seat beside her. Nadia climbed up, sitting next to Khalamoni on the couch.

"Let's come up with some questions together," Khalamoni said.

"Really?" Nadia asked.

"Really! I mean, I had no idea what to ask when I did my very first interview either. It's not always easy to ask the right questions," Khalamoni said.

Nadia nodded. Khalamoni always told her that to be a good journalist, you can't just ask *any* questions; you have to ask the *right* questions. Nadia just didn't know what the right questions were!

"First, to ask the right questions, you have to know the subject of your interview. That's the person, or people, you're interviewing," Khalamoni said.

That made a lot of sense to Nadia. Maybe Nadia had been struggling to come up with questions because she barely knew anything about her subjects!

"So, who are our subjects?" she asked eagerly.

Khalamoni smiled. "Well, they're a family who live in a village in Sylhet. Not *too* far away from here. Their village was affected by floods a few years ago, and a lot of people lost their houses and their farms. This family decided to raise some funds and start a shelter for people who were affected by floods."

Nadia felt sad hearing their story, but it was nice that they had decided to help people from their village. She could already think of questions she wanted to ask them. Like: How did they raise money? What was the flood like? What was the name of their shelter?

She quickly wrote down her questions in her sparkly purple notebook and showed Khalamoni.

"Those are some really good questions, Nadia," Khalamoni said, nodding like she was proud of Nadia. "But there's another step to asking the right questions," Khalamoni said.

"There is?"

"You have to think about how your questions fit into what you're writing about," Khalamoni said. "I'm writing a feature about climate change and the floods in Bangladesh, and how people in Bangladesh are taking action. So, I have to ask questions that help me write that article. If you figure out what you're writing about, that'll help you come up with your own questions. Have you thought more about what you want to write for your article?"

Nadia *had* thought about it, but she still didn't know. There were so many things she *could* write about. She could write about what she was learning about Bangladesh, or the Ramadan race, or about climate change . . . or so many other things!

How would she ever figure out what was the *best* topic to write about so she could become the best editor in chief ever?

When she said all this to Khalamoni, Khalamoni just smiled.

"It's okay, Nadia. It can be difficult to focus on one specific thing to write about. Maybe you just need a little bit more time to figure out what feels exactly right," Khalamoni said.

Maybe she did, but Nadia wished that she could

just think of the perfect idea. She was sure that Khalamoni didn't have to spend a long time coming up with the perfect idea. She always had the best articles.

An hour later, Nadia wandered over to the kitchen table, even though nobody was there. She realized that it was lunch time! Nadia wasn't feeling hungry, really. But she felt like she *should* feel hungry, or that she *should* be eating! It was strange not to have lunch at lunchtime.

"Are you okay, Nadia?" Ammu asked. She was about to take a seat at the dining table with her Qur'an. "Are you feeling hungry?"

"No," Nadia said truthfully. "But it's weird not to be eating lunch right now!"

Ammu smiled. "Our bodies are used to our times for eating meals, so it takes a while to get them to adjust to the Ramadan routine."

Nadia had never thought about how something as simple as fasting means changing your whole routine! As Ammu sat down at the dining table and opened the Qur'an, Nadia took out her sparkly purple notebook and wrote down what Ammu had said. She wondered how long it would take for her body to adjust.

Nadia's first day of Ramadan passed by slowly! She went outside and played with Lily, Rosie, and Adam on the playground for a little bit, but they all grew tired faster than usual. Nadia felt thirsty from the summer heat. Afterward, they came back inside and watched cartoons on the TV. Usually, they would fight over which cartoon to watch, but Nadia felt too sluggish to argue with her brother and cousins for once. So when Adam put on his superhero cartoon, Nadia didn't care!

A little while before iftar, Nanu called all four of them into the kitchen.

"Lily and Rosie, can you make some lemonade for iftar?" Nanu asked.

"Yes, Nanu!" Lily and Rosie said. They sounded like they suddenly had a lot more energy than before. Maybe it was the excitement of finally getting to eat soon.

"Adam and Nadia, why don't you set the table?" Nanu said.

"Okay!" Nadia said.

"Let's see who can do it fastest!" Adam said, nudging Nadia.

Nadia still felt tired from her fast, but there was no way was she going to let Adam beat her at setting the table.

"Okay!" she said.

Adam started setting one side of the table and Nadia started on the other side. They quickly filled the table with placemats, plates, and glasses. They were neck and neck . . . but they got distracted when Mama walked in through the front door carrying canvas bags in both hands.

"Nadia, Adam, give me a hand," he said.

Nadia and Adam looked at each other before abandoning their competition to help Mama. Unlike them, Mama had been at work all day, *and* he was fasting. He must have been exhausted!

"What did you bring?" Nadia asked curiously as she took one of Mama's bags, and Adam took the other.

"Some special sweets for our iftar today," Mama said. "I thought we needed a way to celebrate your very first day of fasting."

Nadia brightened. Bangladeshi sweets were some of her favorites! She couldn't wait to have them when she broke her fast!

"Thanks, Mama!" Nadia said.

Pretty soon, Nadia's whole family sat around the iftar table. The women covered their hair with their urnas, and the men wore tupis. The table was full of delicious Bengali food. There was soft yellow khichuri and spiced chula, along with creamy chicken curry. There was also a plate full of crunchy piyajus and shingaras, beside the boxes of sweets that Mama had brought home as a treat. Creamy roshmalai and juicy-looking kalo jams.

But it wasn't time for them to break fast just yet.

There were still a few minutes to go . . . and Nadia was counting down each second.

"Is it time yet?" Nadia asked.

"Not yet," said Ammu.

"Now?"

"Nadia, it's only been a few seconds," Abbu said impatiently.

Nadia huffed and leaned back in her seat. She was tired and hungry, and all the food on the table looked too good.

Finally, the Maghrib call to prayer came from the mosque down the road. Nadia knew it was time to break her fast. Everybody around the table picked up a date and bit into it. Nadia did too. It tasted delicious! It tasted better than any date she had ever eaten before.

"Why do we break our fast with dates?" Nadia wondered aloud.

"It's because the prophet Mohammad broke his fasts with dates," Abbu replied. "But not everyone does it."

Nadia felt like she was learning a lot about Ramadan and fasting.

Nadia chewed on piyajus and spooned khichuri onto her plate. She ate and ate until she was stuffed! She didn't feel tired or hungry anymore. She felt full and happy.

"Do you want us to wake you up for sehri tomorrow?" Ammu asked Nadia and Adam as they were preparing to go to bed.

The two of them looked at one another. Nadia knew that Lily and Rosie were probably fasting tomorrow. She thought about the interview that she was going to help out with, and how she would have to be out in the heat all day! But . . . she could do it. She would *have* to do it.

"Yes, please!" Nadia said.

"Me too!" Adam agreed.

"Are you sure you can handle it?"

"One hundred percent!" said Nadia enthusiastically.

"One thousand percent!" said Adam.

Ammu laughed. "Okay, okay. I'll wake you both up for sehri."

"Can I have the window side of the bed today?" Nadia asked Adam once Ammu was gone. That was the side where the breeze came in and it was cooler. Adam had been sleeping on that side every day.

"No way, that's *my* side of the bed," Adam said. He was already crawling toward it. Nadia huffed. Normally, she would challenge Adam to some kind of competition to see who got that side of the bed, but she was tired from her day of fasting. Plus, she knew she would have to wake up for sehri soon.

CHAPTER 13

A Ramadan to Remember

"Nadia, it's almost time to get going!" Khalamoni's voice woke Nadia up. "Do you still want to go?"

Nadia sat up in bed, still groggy from sleep. She felt like she had just woken up for sehri, though she could barely remember that, and now it was time to wake up again!

"I still want to go," Nadia mumbled, though she was half asleep.

"Are you sure?"

Nadia shook herself awake. She couldn't let Khalamoni doubt her, and she didn't want to miss her very first interview.

"Yes, I'm sure!" Nadia said, jumping out of bed

so Khalamoni could see just how sure she really was. She looked at Khalamoni, who already looked ready. Ever since coming to Bangladesh, she had swapped puffy blouses and jeans for simple cotton salwar kameezes. She said that it helped with the heat, and she had even bought a few for Nadia. Today, Khalamoni wore a blue-and-white salwar kameez, and she had brushed her hair into a long ponytail.

"We're leaving in thirty minutes, okay? Make sure you wear something comfortable. It's hot out today." Khalamoni gave Nadia a comforting smile, but Nadia's stomach churned with nervousness. She had heard stories from Khalamoni about interviews, but she had never sat in on an interview or had the chance to help Khalamoni with something like this. Today was her chance to prove herself, and Nadia had to make the most of it.

Khalamoni was right—it was scorching hot outside, even with Nadia wearing one of the cotton salwar kameezes Khalamoni had bought her. Nadia and Khalamoni sped through the city in a CNG.

"Will it take us long to get there?" Nadia asked, though she wasn't sure if Khalamoni could hear her over the loud rumble of the CNG's engine.

"Just a little more time," Khalamoni responded, though she was looking through the pages of a folder in her hands instead of at Nadia. Khalamoni had been quiet throughout this entire journey, and it made Nadia even more nervous than usual. She looked outside at the buildings and people zooming by, until the CNG turned right into a quieter road and seemed to zip out of the city altogether. Instead of buildings, Nadia could see fields, farmland, tin huts, and long stretches of water with boats bobbing on them. It was a side of Bangladesh that Nadia hadn't seen before now. She turned to ask Khalamoni more questions, but she was still busy, and Nadia didn't want to interrupt her.

Finally, the CNG pulled up by the side of a relatively secluded road. There was a narrow path that led down to a pond, which was surrounded by a series of tin houses.

"Is this still Sylhet?" Nadia asked once Khalamoni had paid the CNG driver.

"Yes, but not Sylhet city anymore," Khalamoni said. "Come on."

She led Nadia past the pond and up a long flight of clay steps. There was a house at the very top of the steps, overlooking the rest of the village. It was bigger than some of the other houses they had passed, almost double the size.

Khalamoni walked onto the porch and knocked on the front door three times before it swung open.

A man and woman stood at the doorway, smiles on both their faces. The man wore a plain white panjabi, while the woman wore a plain black saree.

"Ms. Islam?" the man asked.

"Yes, that's me," Khalamoni said with a nod. "And this is my niece, Nadia."

"Assalam alaikum. I'm Asifa, and this is my husband, Reyhan," the woman—Asifa Auntie—said.

"Walaikum salam," replied Nadia and Khalamoni.

"Come in, come in." They stepped aside as Nadia and Khalamoni entered the house. Even though it had looked a little old and worn down from the outside, the inside of the house was big and spacious. Nadia and Khalamoni were standing in the front entrance, which led to a large sitting room filled with furniture made from cane.

"This way!" The man and woman led Nadia and Khalamoni to the sitting room. There was already a girl there—not much older than Nadia. She wore a pink salwar kameez with flower patterns and had an urna wrapped around her head. It wasn't the way some of the aunties back home wore their hijabs, wrapped tight and covering every inch of hair. In fact, it wasn't really a hijab at all. Nadia had noticed that a lot of people in Bangladesh loosely covered their hair with urnas.

"Assalam alaikum," the girl said in a soft voice.

"Walaikum salam!" Nadia said. She was happy that there was someone around her own age here, instead of just adults.

Asifa Auntie and Reyhan Uncle sat down on either side of the girl, while Khalamoni and Nadia sat on a couch opposite them.

"This is our daughter, Reem," Reyhan Uncle said, introducing the girl on the couch between them.

"Hi, Reem. It's nice to meet you! I'm Nadia!" Nadia said before anybody else could. She suddenly wondered if she had spoken out of turn and slunk back in her seat, feeling shy. Khalamoni had said this was going to be a professional interview.

"Yes, it's nice to meet you, Reem," Khalamoni said.

"It's nice to meet you too," said Reem. Her voice was still quiet, but she didn't seem shy.

Khalamoni opened her notebook, and then it was all business. Nadia opened her notebook too, though she wasn't sure exactly what she was going to write in it.

"So, as you know, I'm writing a feature about Bangladesh, climate change, and how the people here are dealing with it. I read about what happened to your village and how you helped your neighbors here. And how you've even built a shelter to help house climate refugees." Khalamoni took out her phone and added, "Do you mind if I record our conversation?"

Asifa Auntie and Reyhan Uncle shared a look, before shaking their heads no at Khalamoni's question.

"Well, we're really happy that you're writing about our village and what happened here. But really, I think you should be speaking to Reem," Asifa Auntie said.

Khalamoni looked at Auntie and Uncle, confused. But Nadia looked at Reem. She seemed to have a quiet confidence about her that Nadia liked. It reminded her a little of Yasmin. Everyone always said that Yasmin was quiet, and sometimes they said that she was shy, especially compared to Nadia! But Nadia knew Yasmin was quiet and confident, and really smart and an amazing friend! She wondered if Reem was like that too.

"Reem? She was involved?" Khalamoni asked.

Reyhan Uncle nodded. "More than involved. She was the one who came to us with the ideas for everything. Really, all we did was provide some financial support. Everything else was her."

Khalamoni's eyes widened at that, and she looked from Uncle and Auntie to Reem.

"That's amazing!" Nadia said. She couldn't believe that someone close to her age could actually do something to make a difference.

"Yes, Nadia's right. That *is* amazing. How old are you, Reem?" Khalamoni asked.

"I'm twelve years old," Reem replied. "But I was ten when I got the idea to open a shelter, using the house that belonged to my grandparents."

"Can you tell me what happened?" Khalamoni asked.

Reem nodded and took a deep breath. "Flooding has always been a problem around here, but a few years ago, we had a big flood that affected our village. A lot of people lost their homes, and some people lost their livelihoods. I thought . . . when things like that happen, people come to help. I'd seen it in the news, or read about it. But it was just us, really, and nobody was coming to help. We had a small community here and we helped each other out. My ammu and abbu helped some people find shelters in another village. Some of my family from the city came down to help people rebuild. But . . . as you probably saw, our village was never really the same again. Some people couldn't rebuild and some people decided to just . . . leave."

"That sounds terrible," Khalamoni said, shaking her head.

Nadia was trying to imagine all of it. She was having a hard time. She had never even heard of a situation like that before. She wondered what the village used to be like before the flood changed things.

But . . . she had questions too.

"What does that have to do with climate change?" Nadia blurted out.

Reem turned to look at Nadia, but she didn't look annoyed at the question. She looked like she was almost taking Nadia seriously.

"The flood made me learn about why it had happened. Before that, I never knew that Bangladesh is one of the most climate-vulnerable countries. That's why we have such terrible floods, and it's why they seem to get worse and worse as time goes on," Reem said. "But I also never knew that things are even worse on our coasts, where sea-water is rising and our land is going underwater."

Khalamoni was nodding along to Reem's words and writing down notes in her notepad, but Nadia could only blink at Reem, trying to take it all in. Shouldn't everyone be talking about it if this was really happening?

"So . . . you decided to take matters into your own hands?" Khalamoni asked encouragingly.

"Yes. I knew that someone had to do *something*. I wanted to help our neighbors, and I wanted to help people who were in similar situations as us. I went to my ammu and abbu with my idea for setting up a shelter of our own, and then I went online to raise funds and awareness of what was happening. A lot of people came onto the project, but a lot of people also told me that I should just leave it. I was only ten years old at the time, and they thought someone my age couldn't do anything. That I didn't even understand what was happening, really. But it was my village that had been harmed, my friends and family. People that I knew. I couldn't just sit by and do nothing."

Nadia could hardly believe it. Reem was only ten years old when she'd learned all of this? That was only two years older than Nadia now!

It seemed to Nadia that Reem and she had more in common than she had first realized, but that Reem and she were so different too. Nadia and Reem both struggled to be taken seriously . . . but Reem had proved everyone wrong. The fact that this interview was happening was proof of that.

"How did you do it?" Nadia asked in awe.

Reem smiled at her again, and Nadia almost felt like they had known each other for a long time. Like they were friends.

"It was a lot of hard work. I can tell you both about it, but it would be . . . better if I could show you everything." For the first time since the interview started, Reem glanced at her parents, like she was asking for their permission.

"We'll have to check with the residents at the shelter. I'm sure they'll be fine with it," Reem's mom said. "Why don't you come back tomorrow afternoon?"

Khalamoni nodded. "We can come tomorrow. We should be getting home now, to make it in time for iftar."

Nadia didn't want to leave. She wanted to ask more questions, learn more about Reem and everything that she was doing. But with the mention of iftar, it was like a spell had broken. Nadia's stomach rumbled hungrily, and her throat suddenly felt dry.

"Come on, Nadia. We'll be back again. We still have a lot of work to do," Khalamoni said.

Nadia didn't want their conversation to end. "I'm going to write an article in my school newspaper about everything I learn in Bangladesh,"

Nadia said to Reem, her voice low as if it was a secret between the two of them. "Everyone thinks that I'm a baby, but I want to prove them wrong with my journalism, like you proved everyone wrong with your activism."

Reem beamed at Nadia, like she understood exactly what Nadia was talking about. "That's amazing, Nadia," she said encouragingly. "I bet you're a really great journalist."

Nadia and Reem exchanged their email addresses before finally saying goodbye. Nadia still had a lot of questions for Reem and maybe now she could ask some of them!

By the time Nadia and Khalamoni arrived home, it was almost time for iftar. Nadia felt exhausted— even more tired than she had felt yesterday! Nadia had thought fasting was supposed to get easier, but fasting today seemed even harder than the day before.

"Are you doing okay, Nadia?" Khalamoni asked after the two of them were indoors and being cooled by the AC in the sitting room.

"I'm okay. I'm just tired," Nadia said. She was too tired to even think about lying and saying she was fine!

Khalamoni gave Nadia a sympathetic smile. "Do you want to break your fast? There's still a few hours until iftar."

Nadia almost said yes, but then she remembered the Ramadan race. She couldn't break her fast.

"No, thank you," Nadia said.

"Why don't you take a nap, then? I'll make sure to wake you up when it's time for iftar."

That sounded like a better idea. Nadia shuffled to the bedroom and found Adam already asleep on his side of the bed. She was glad to see that at least she wasn't the only one tired from all the fasting!

"Nadia!" Lily called to her from the sitting room after iftar. Abbu, Mama, and Adam had gone to the mosque to pray isha and taraweeh.

Nadia came out of her bedroom, where she had been writing in her notebook about everything she'd learned today—from Reem all the way to her first iftar while fasting.

"What?" Nadia asked.

Lily and Rosie were sitting together, eating from a box of jilapis. Almost all of the jilapis were already gone. They definitely had a sweet tooth, but Nadia couldn't blame them. Jilapis were probably the most delicious sweets in the world—and Ramadan was the perfect excuse to eat as many of them as you could.

"We have an amazing idea for how to win the Ramadan race," Rosie said, patting the seat next to her on the couch for Nadia to sit on.

Nadia frowned but sat down next to Rosie. "But I thought we were competing against each other."

"Yes, but . . . maybe it should be boys vs. girls first," Rosie said. "Lily and I think so."

Lily nodded, like she definitely agreed. Nadia

wasn't so sure. Adam was her older brother, and he could be really annoying. But making the race boys vs. girls when Adam was the only boy seemed really unfair.

"I just think that it'll make things easier for you, since you're the youngest of all of us," Rosie added.

Nadia frowned even more. "I don't need extra help! I fasted yesterday and today without any problems."

"That was today and yesterday," Rosie said. "What about tomorrow? Don't you already feel tired?"

Nadia *did* feel tired. And tomorrow they were going to visit Reem again, so she could show them the work she had done. But Nadia wouldn't let Rosie and Lily win. And she definitely couldn't let Adam win.

"I'll be fine," Nadia said. "I can do it on my own, with no help." But Nadia wasn't as confident as she pretended to be. She would have to find some way to beat Adam and her cousins.

NADIA ISLAM'S INVESTIGATIVE QUESTIONS ABOUT CLIMATE CHANGE

Question #1: Bangladesh has a *lot* of floods! There are floods almost every year! Why is that the case?

Question #2: In school, we learned about the melting ice caps in Antarctica. But Bangladesh is so far away from Antarctica. Are the melting ice caps somehow causing floods in Bangladesh?!

Question #3: From the project about water that Yasmin and I did, we learned that we should use less water to help the climate! What can we do to help stop climate change in Bangladesh?!

Climate Change Wreaks Havoc on Bangladesh . . . and Nadia Sees It All!

Nadia was even more tired when Khalamoni woke her up the next day. She felt like she could barely open her eyes and see the blurry Khalamoni shape in front of her. Still, she somehow rolled out of bed, yawning wide and for what felt like a really long time.

"I can go on my own today, if you feel too tired from fasting," Khalamoni said when she saw how slow Nadia was to get ready.

"No!" Nadia mumbled, wishing that she didn't feel as tired as she did. "I can go, promise. I'm not tired at all!"

"Hmm." Khalamoni didn't look like she believed Nadia, but she didn't say anything else.

Khalamoni had hired a car this time around. It was great, especially since it had been raining since last night. The two of them piled into the car, and Nadia pressed her face to the windows throughout the journey. It was a shorter trip than it would have been on the CNG, but it was just as bumpy!

Reem and her parents were waiting for Nadia in the foyer of their house. Reem's face broke out into a smile when she saw them, and Nadia waved. She felt like she and Reem were old friends, even though they'd only just met. It was a strange feeling, but it was also how she had felt when she had first met Yasmin. They were seated next to each other in school, and when the teacher asked a question in class, Yasmin was always quick to answer. Nadia had liked that about her. After class, she had asked Yasmin a million questions, and it was clear that they had so much in common they were destined to be best friends. She had a million questions for Reem now too.

"We got a car and a driver to bring us to the shelter," Khalamoni said. "Probably the easiest thing in the rain."

Reem and her parents piled into the car and then the driver was off. Reem's mom gave the driver instructions as they pulled out of Reem's village. They went down a winding road, and Nadia could see water in the distance. Her mouth dropped open because they weren't very far from the city.

"There is flooding out here?" Nadia asked.

Reem nodded her head sadly. "The worst of it is gone, but it's still not great. Only some of the city was hit, and it could have been much worse. But a lot of the villages have been destroyed."

They kept driving, and the farther they went, the worse it seemed to get. Nadia saw entire fields filled with water. If she didn't know about the flooding, she might have just thought it was a small lake on the side of the road. But she knew better now. She wondered what happened to the people who owned these lands.

They drove past a few villages where Nadia could see the damage that the floods had done. She didn't just see fields filled with water, but also homes that had been destroyed, as well as rickshaws, CNGs, and cars in ruins. In one village, there was even a small school that had water on the first floor, and water damage to its outside walls. She wondered where the students would study once the summer vacation was over.

Finally, the car drove up a steep hill and parked near a row of interconnected houses in another village. Outside the double doors, a sign read, "The Talukdar Shelter." Everyone got out of the car, and Reem led them all indoors.

The rooms inside were modest, nothing like the houses Nadia was used to. There were a few single bedframes pushed against the walls, but mostly there were mattresses made into makeshift beds on the floor. There were women resting on the beds, their children by their sides. They looked tired, much more tired than Nadia felt. There was one woman in the corner of the room praying on a jainamaz, and another beside her on a mattress muttering prayers while counting prayer beads.

"As you can see, we're struggling to properly house people here," Reem said in a low voice so as to not disturb all the women in the house. "Our shelter is only for women and their children for now, because they've been hit the hardest by the floods. It's sad to sometimes have to split up families. But we don't have proper beds here, and there's only one bathroom that everyone has to share. This was just a house that belonged to my grandparents that we decided to convert into a shelter. That's why we're lacking facilities. We're trying to raise money to build something better. We were even in Dhaka last week, meeting with people who may be able to help us raise some funds and trying to see if we could build a house there, since a capital city has more job opportunities."

Khalamoni nodded as Reem spoke, writing

everything down in her notebook.

"Do you mind if we speak to some of these women?" Khalamoni asked.

Reem shook her head. "Just . . . be respectful. They've been through a lot."

Khalamoni nodded and led Nadia over to the woman who had been praying just a moment ago. She was now folding up her prayer mat to put away.

"Hi," Khalamoni said. "I'm a journalist writing about Reem, her work with climate change, and what's happening in Bangladesh right now. I was wondering if I could ask you a few questions."

The woman looked from Khalamoni to Nadia. Then, she slowly nodded.

"Okay, great. What's your name?"

"Jawaria Chowdhury," she said.

"Jawaria . . ." Khalamoni mumbled as she scribbled the name down. "Can you tell me a little about how you came to this shelter?"

"I worked as a maid for one of the families in

Sylhet city, but my home was in a village near here. I have a little one just like yours. . . ."

She nodded at Nadia, and Khalamoni didn't correct her to say Nadia was her niece, not her daughter. Not that Nadia minded.

"When the floods started getting bad, I was home with my daughter. The water had risen high enough that we weren't sure how to leave our village. I had to get to work, and my daughter had school, but unless we swam there, there was no way we would make it. A few people from this shelter came the next day on boats. We took whatever belongings weren't damaged and got on the boats. They brought us here, and we've been here since. The family I was working for let me go because I didn't show up for work for a few days, so now I'm looking for something new."

"That's horrible!" Nadia blurted out. "Didn't they know about the floods?"

Jawaria smiled down at Nadia, even though there was nothing to smile about. "They knew, but . . . I guess they were more worried about having someone to cook and clean for them than what was happening to us."

Nadia couldn't believe anybody could be so mean.

"Do you think this shelter helped you?" Khala-moni asked.

"Yes, definitely. Without the shelter, I'm not sure where my family would be right now. They've given us a place to stay and made sure we have food in our bellies. Especially through Ramadan when we're all fasting, and it's even harder than usual."

Nadia felt her stomach twist with discomfort. Even with the floods and losing her home, Jawaria was fasting through Ramadan. She wasn't sure why learning that made her feel weird.

"And Reem has been helping me look for a new job too. She and her family have been searching for anyone looking for a maid, especially some-one who can stay with the family. Once they find someone suitable, I'll have a more permanent place to stay and a job to save up money for our family," Jawaria continued with a grin.

"Thank you, Jawaria. It was really great speaking to you today," Khalamoni said. She took down Jawaria's details and her permission to use her name in her newspaper article. Khalamoni and Nadia spoke to a few more people around the shelter. They all had stories similar to Jawaria's, about how they'd lost so much to the floods. That was why they'd had to come here. Now, they were looking for a more permanent place and jobs.

On the way back to Reem's village, Nadia and Reem sat side by side in the back of the car. Nadia had so many questions for Reem that she didn't even know what she should ask.

"How did you get the idea for the shelter?" Nadia had been curious about this. She would never have thought of something like that, even though it made perfect sense.

Reem shrugged. "I don't know. When my grandparents were alive, me and my family used to go to that house all the time, but ever since they passed away, it's been left unused. At first, I thought about maybe letting some of our neighbors stay there while they figured things out, but it grew into something bigger fast."

"Wow," said Nadia.

"It was difficult, though. The house needed repairs, so we had to do a lot of fundraising and even put up a lot of our own money. People don't always want to help."

Nadia felt sad about that, but she knew it was true. Fundraising wasn't always easy. "In school, when we want to fundraise for something, we always have a bake sale. My friend Yasmin loves art, but the art classes in our school didn't have a lot of money for new supplies, so they had a bake sale to buy new paintbrushes and paint and easels. My mom helped me make chocolate chip cookies for it. Maybe you should have a bake sale too."

Reem grinned. "I love chocolate chip cookies.

But I think a bake sale is too small. It takes a lot of money to fix a house, to pay the bills, and have enough food for everyone at the shelter. And it's not a one-time thing like painting supplies."

Nadia understood that. The painting supplies that Yasmin's art class had bought would probably last them years. But Abbu needed to do the grocery shopping for their house twice a week. And Ammu paid the bills every single month!

Even though Nadia's idea wasn't very helpful, Reem didn't seem to mind. She asked Nadia questions about her town, her school, journalism, and even Yasmin. Nadia was all too happy to answer. It was strange how at ease Nadia felt when the two of them were talking. Reem didn't make Nadia feel like a baby even though she was way older than Nadia.

By the time they had dropped Reem off at her house and were on the way back home, Nadia was tired and hungry, and there were still ages left until iftar. She took out her notebook and tried to jot down notes about everything that she was learning and seeing, but she could barely focus. Instead, she thought about how parched she felt, and how dry her throat was. She didn't know tiredness could make it difficult to think!

"When will it be sundown?" Nadia asked Khalamoni.

"It's only one p.m., Nadia. There's still five hours left," Khalamoni said.

Nadia groaned, sitting back in her seat and closing her eyes. Her stomach let out a loud rumble that echoed around the silent car. Nadia felt her face heat up and, when she opened her eyes, Khalamoni was looking at her with sympathy on her face.

"Are you sure you don't want to break your fast?" Khalamoni asked.

"But I've fasted for this long . . ." Nadia mumbled. She was sure she could do five more hours. But she was *so* hungry. She had been out and about all day.

"And you've had a really long day. One day off from fasting won't be a big deal. And if you eat now, it'll be just like you're having your lunch after a really early breakfast."

When Khalamoni put it like that, it made Nadia feel better. It was a little like that.

But then she remembered the Ramadan race. She was pretty sure that Adam and her cousins weren't going to break their fasts. If she broke hers, she would lose, and that would mean they were right about her. That she was a baby who couldn't keep as many fasts as they could. Not to mention that it would mean she wouldn't be able to have fun with Adam and her cousins on Eid . . . which would ruin it!

"I can do it; I can keep fasting," Nadia insisted, even though her stomach lurched with hunger. Nadia always heard stories about fasting being difficult, but she'd never thought it would be this difficult! How did the adults fast for thirty whole days?

"Nadia, don't be silly," Khalamoni said. "Come on, we're getting you some food."

"But . . ." Nadia almost blurted out the truth about the Ramadan race, but stopped herself at the last minute.

"It's your first time fasting and you're doing amazing," Khalamoni said as she directed the driver to change directions. "The first time I tried to fast, I couldn't even go the whole day."

Nadia's eyes widened. "Really?" She thought Khalamoni was the kind of person who could do anything she set her mind to.

"Really." Khalamoni nodded. "I was younger than you, and I was desperate to keep up with your ammu and mama, but . . . I just couldn't handle it. I started crying from how hungry I was, and your nanu told me that I had to break my fast. I was glad that I did. You'll be glad that you did too."

The car pulled up to a small restaurant in the city, and when Nadia smelled the delicious scent of food from indoors, her hunger just grew and grew.

"Order anything you want. My treat for all your hard work today," Khalamoni said.

Nadia looked at the menu and all the delicious food options, but she couldn't bring herself to order anything. If she broke her fast, wouldn't she be admitting to Adam and Lily and Rosie that they were right about her?

"Come on, Nadia. You can't be a good journalist if you're not at your best," Khalamoni said. "Get your energy back, and you'll be helping me immensely."

Nadia thought about it for a moment, but she didn't think *too* hard. She knew Khalamoni wouldn't let this go, and she was *so* hungry. Maybe breaking one fast wouldn't be a big deal. She could still win the Ramadan race; she knew she could. She ordered a chicken burger and fries, along with a giant bottle of water which she gulped down quickly. Relief flooded through her. She hadn't even realized just how thirsty she was, especially since the sun was up high and heat prickled her skin. The heat in Bangladesh was like no other.

Nadia felt a little bad about breaking her fast, but when her burger was ready and she took a bite, those feelings slowly disappeared.

Nadia Takes a Break

When Nadia and Khalamoni arrived home, there was chaos everywhere! Lily was crying and being soothed by her mom, while Rosie and Adam were having a huge argument that Ammu and Mama were trying to break up.

"What's going on here?" Khalamoni asked as she and Nadia slipped through the front door. Nadia felt like she had stepped into a completely different world, away from the shelter and all of Reem's work and into a life where only her chaotic family existed.

"Lily and Rosie were trying to make me break my fast. They wanted to play hide-and-seek outside, and I was running everywhere looking for them in the heat until I was too tired and thirsty! And they were inside all along, not even really playing the game!" Adam cried. His voice already sounded hoarse.

"I can't believe you'd accuse us like that!" Rosie cried, while Lily wailed loudly in the corner.

"Adam, if you feel too tired, you can always break—"

"No! I don't want to." Adam crossed his arms stubbornly.

"Nadia broke her fast today, and it wasn't a big deal," Khalamoni added.

Nadia wished she hadn't, because then *everybody* turned to look at her. Even Lily, whose wails had turned into sniffles all of a sudden. Nadia felt heat rush up her face.

"You did?" Rosie asked. She sounded delighted about it, and it made Nadia wish she hadn't broken her fast.

"I'm glad!" Ammu declared. "Nadia was out all day helping her khalamoni. It's not easy to fast under those circumstances. There's no shame in having to break your fast. Allah allows it. Fasting is meant to be a challenge, but not one you can't handle."

The rest of the adults nodded in agreement, but Nadia still felt a little ashamed. Mostly, she felt embarrassed that she was the one to break first. She thought for sure it would be Adam.

But Khalamoni's reveal meant the fight finally came to an end. Still, Ammu seemed to be taking it all very seriously.

"Tomorrow, all of you are taking a day off from fasting," she declared.

"But we don't need to!" Rosie said.

"We don't *want* to!" Lily agreed.

"I agree," Mama said with a decisive nod. "It's good that all of you are excited about fasting, but clearly, it's been hard. It's time to take a day off."

Nadia felt a jolt of excitement. Maybe this meant she wouldn't be dead last in the Ramadan race after all. She had broken her fast today, so she could still fast tomorrow.

"And that includes you, Nadia," Ammu said, looking right at her like she knew what Nadia had been thinking.

"But I broke my fast today!" Nadia said.

Ammu shook her head. "That doesn't matter. Tomorrow, none of you are fasting, and that's final."

No matter how much they insisted, Mama and Ammu wouldn't give in, and even Khalamoni agreed with them. Eventually, Adam grumbled about being too tired from running around outside and went off into their bedroom to take a nap, while the adults went into the kitchen to prepare iftar.

"Even if we're not allowed to fast tomorrow, you're still losing," Rosie said with a grin once the adults were out of earshot.

"Not for long!" Nadia said, even though she didn't feel very confident about it.

"If you want a chance to win, you're going to have to help us sabotage Adam," Lily said. So

Adam was right—Lily and Rosie *had* tried to get him to break his fast.

"Adam is really stubborn. He won't break his fast that easy," Nadia said. Adam could do anything that he set his mind to—something Nadia and he had in common, according to their parents. But Nadia knew Adam's weaknesses too.

Still, she hesitated to share what she knew with Lily and Rosie. Did she really want to make Adam break his fast? When she beat Adam at their races, she always did it fair and square, and this didn't feel like it would be fair or square.

But Nadia knew that Lily and Rosie were right. Nadia had to find some way to catch up on the Ramadan race, and maybe the only way to do that was to sabotage Adam.

The next day, Nadia didn't wake up at dawn to eat sehri. Instead, she woke up at ten in the morning, feeling rested and happy. Adam was already awake too, playing video games in the sitting room with Lily and Rosie. And even though they were all pretending to be grumpy about not being allowed to fast, Nadia knew that they were feeling better too. The four of them spent the day eating meals as usual (which felt unusual after just three days of fasting)! They played outside together and even walked to the corner shop to buy spicy Bangladeshi crisps as an afternoon snack.

"You can take a few more days off from fasting, if you want," Mama said to the four of them during iftar that day. "You'll have more energy to play together and enjoy your summer."

Nadia almost wanted to say yes, please! She liked fasting even though it was tiring, but she also liked having fun with her cousins. Maybe more than she liked always competing with them. It was fun to compete sometimes but not *all* the time. She looked to Lily and Rosie to see what they would say, but they just shook their heads.

"We're too old to skip so many fasts!" Rosie said.

"And we're too mature to spend all our time playing anyway," said Lily in agreement.

Mama sighed. "If you're sure," he said.

"What about you two?" Ammu said, turning to Nadia and Adam.

"I . . . also want to keep fasting," said Nadia quickly. She couldn't back down from the Ramadan race, not now.

"Me too!" agreed Adam.

"Okay, but remember what we said before. All of you need to take it easy during Ramadan. It's okay to take a break every once in a while," Ammu said. "Actually, it's *good* to take a break. It's healthy for you."

"But you never take a break," Nadia pointed out.

"Because I'm an adult, Nadia," Ammu explained. "When I was your age, I couldn't keep as many fasts. I usually kept one and then had to skip the next one."

Mama laughed and added, "And if school was on? Your ammu always struggled to fast then. She

172

barely kept any fasts during that time."

Ammu glared at Mama, and it reminded Nadia of her and Adam, always teasing each other. It almost looked like Mama would stick his tongue out at Ammu, like Adam did with Nadia! But he didn't; he just smiled at Ammu and shrugged, and then Ammu laughed too.

"Yeah, I always struggled to fast during school time, you're right. But you weren't much better!" she said.

Nadia wondered if all brothers and sisters were like Nadia and Adam, always teasing each other and competing. Or maybe it was just the Islams!

Nadia Pulls a Prank!

When Nadia woke up the next morning, she was full of energy. The break from fasting had recharged her. It had even given her an idea for how she could sabotage Adam. She tiptoed toward the bedroom Lily and Rosie shared, making sure that she wouldn't disturb Adam in his sleep. Outside the door there was a sign in red that said "KEEP OUT," and two little blackboard signs. One sign had Lily's name on it in pretty cursive handwriting with doodles of lilies and stars surrounding it. The other had the name Rosie in a similar but slightly different handwriting and had doodles of roses, thorns, and stems.

Nadia knocked on the door. No sound. In fact,

the entire house was silent. Like Nadia was the first one awake!

Nadia opened the door a crack and peeked inside. Lily and Rosie were asleep on their beds on opposite sides of the room. They didn't look so scary when they were sleeping, but as older cousins, they seemed more intimidating to Nadia when awake.

"Lily! Rosie!" Nadia called to wake them up. Lily stirred a little in her sleep, but Rosie didn't move at all.

"*Lily! Rosie!* If you don't wake up, we can't win the Ramadan race!" Nadia cried. This jolted both of them out of their sleep. Lily sat up, rubbing sleep out of her eyes, while Rosie stretched her arms over her head and yawned wide.

"Okay, okay. We're awake. What do you want?" Rosie asked.

"I have an idea for how we can make Adam break his fast!" Nadia said. "But we have to go to the shop to get something first."

Lily and Rosie looked at Nadia with raised eyebrows until she explained exactly what her plan was and why it would work.

Then, the two of them got dressed, said goodbye to Mami, and led Nadia out of the house. This was Nadia's first time really being alone with her two cousins, and it felt weird. Nadia hadn't even known her cousins before she came to Bangladesh, and now she was teaming up with them to beat Adam in the Ramadan race.

"What have you been doing with Chuto Fufu these past two days?" Rosie asked curiously as they walked down the gravel path. Chuto Fufu was what Rosie and Lily called Nadia's khalamoni.

"I'm helping her with her journalism," Nadia said. "I want to be a journalist too."

"You're too little to help her," Rosie said, but Lily elbowed her in the stomach.

"Don't be rude. Nadia isn't *that* small. And she *has been* going out with Chuto Fufu all the time,"

Lily said. Nadia was surprised that Lily defended her against her sister.

"I'm going to write all about my experiences in Bangladesh, and it's going to be in my school newspaper," Nadia said with a huff. "And I'll even write about how I won the Ramadan race."

Rosie didn't look like she believed Nadia, but she said, "We'll see. Let's try and get Adam to break a fast first."

The three of them turned into the footpath off the main road. There were rickshaws and CNGs nestled by the sides of the road, and so many people walking and talking. Nadia wasn't used to such busy streets. It was a little overwhelming, but Nadia was coming to enjoy these things about Bangladesh that she didn't experience in her small town at home.

Lily and Rosie led Nadia to a sweet shop at the end of the street. The shop had a colorful sign on top in Bengali letters that Nadia couldn't read.

"It's Bonoful," Rosie said when she saw Nadia

squinting up at the sign.

"I know that," Nadia said, even though she hadn't. But she knew that Bonoful was a popular sweet shop in Bangladesh.

They entered the shop and Nadia was amazed at the rows and rows of all different kinds of sweets. There was even a small corner of the shop dedicated to American candy. Nadia wasn't interested in that when she had Bengali sweets to entice her brother.

"Are you sure this will work?" Rosie asked as Nadia picked out a box of mishti with different kinds of sweets.

"Adam has the biggest sweet tooth ever," Nadia said. "It *has* to work."

By the time Nadia and her two cousins arrived home from the sweet shop, almost everyone in the house was awake. Nanu was in her bedroom, reading the Qur'an, Mama was at work, Mami was reading a book, Khalamoni was on her laptop doing research, while Nadia's ammu and abbu watched the news in the sitting room.

Nadia said hello to her parents, hiding her box of sweets behind her back. They were so distracted by the news that they didn't even ask Nadia any questions.

Nadia slipped into the bedroom she was sharing with Adam. He was nowhere to be found! After a moment, Nadia heard the sound of running water coming from their bathroom. It had to be Adam, taking a shower. This was her perfect chance.

She took the box of Adam's favorite mishtis and placed them on the bedside table. She opened up the box so the sweet scent would fill the entire room, and then Adam would have no choice but to break his fast.

"Write a note!" Rosie whispered from the bedroom doorway where she and Lily watched.

"To say what?" Nadia asked as she looked around for a pen and some paper.

"Something to tell him that the mishtis are

from your parents or Nanu . . . so he doesn't get suspicious!" Lily said.

That was a pretty good idea, Nadia thought. She finally found a notebook and a pencil in one of the bedside drawers and scribbled out a note that read, "Dear Adam, we got you this box of mishtis because we're so proud of you for fasting this year. Love, Ammu and Abbu."

Nadia grinned down at the note, feeling pretty proud of herself. When Adam saw the note and the box of mishtis, he would *have* to have one. And then Nadia wouldn't be dead last anymore.

The sound of the running shower stopped in the bathroom, so Nadia placed the note right beside the open box and hurried outside of the room.

She waited by the bedroom door with Lily and Rosie. They watched as the bathroom door opened and Adam walked out, freshly showered. He spotted the box of mishtis almost immediately, and his eyes widened. He looked around like he was confused, and Nadia and her cousins ducked out of sight. If they were spotted, their plans would be ruined right there and then.

When they glanced up again, Adam was closing the lid of the box. He hadn't taken a single bite!

Rosie turned to Nadia with a glare. "I thought you said this would work."

"I thought it would. . . ." Nadia said. She had been so sure Adam wouldn't be able to resist.

Nadia marched over to Adam with her hands on her hips. She needed answers.

"What are you doing? Ammu and Abbu got you that entire box of mishtis, and you're not going to have any?" Nadia asked.

"I can't. I'm fasting. I'll eat them after iftar," Adam said with a shrug. Nadia could see the smug smile he was hiding, though.

"These are your favorite mishtis, and iftar is so far away. Are you sure you can wait all that time?" Nadia asked.

"I'm sure," Adam said with a grin. "Ammu and Abbu told me yesterday that when we fast for

Ramadan, we're learning self-control. I have so much self-control that I don't have to eat these mishtis right away."

Nadia blinked at Adam in confusion. She had heard her parents talk about how Ramadan was about more than fasting. It made sense that it was about self-control. Nadia had to have self-control in the mishti shop not to gobble up her favorites too. She had to have self-control on the days she was fasting so as to not break her fast.

Nadia just didn't know when Adam had become so grown-up, and when he had learned all of this self-control!

But then Adam stuck out his tongue at Nadia and said, "Besides, I know it was you, Lily, and Rosie who got me the mishtis. I know your handwriting, and I can see Lily and Rosie by the doorway."

Lily and Rosie groaned from the door as Adam put away the mishtis happily.

Nadia hadn't managed to get Adam to break a

fast . . . she had just secured him a treat to look forward to instead!

She would have to find some other way to beat Adam, and Lily and Rosie too.

Nadia Observes an Amazing Photo Shoot!

After iftar that day, Khalamoni told Nadia that tomorrow she had arranged to do a quick photoshoot with Reem outside the shelter she'd built.

A photo shoot! Nadia had never been at a photo shoot before.

"I asked one of my friends in Sylhet if they would take the photos. I think it'll really help bring the article together. Hopefully the newspaper who accepted the pitch will like all the work I've put into it!" Khalamoni said brightly. Sometimes when Khalamoni talked about freelancing, she sounded dejected. She talked about how she had to work without the promise of getting paid (which Nadia still didn't completely understand) and how she was always chasing invoices (and then Khalamoni had to explain exactly what an invoice was). But with this article, Khalamoni had only ever sounded hopeful and happy. Nadia could tell this article meant a lot to Khalamoni. It meant a lot to Nadia as well.

"I want to come!" Nadia said, jumping up and down with excitement.

But the next morning, when Nadia's alarm sounded, she was still sleepy! It felt like sehri had been just minutes ago! Still, she got out of bed and got ready. She couldn't miss the photo shoot!

As soon as Khalamoni and Nadia were on the road, Nadia realized she had made a huge mistake. It was already so hot, and Khalamoni's photo shoot idea meant that they'd probably be out in the sun for the whole day. Nadia couldn't break her fast again. Adam, Lily, and Rosie were fasting today too, and so if she broke her fast, she would never catch up with them, no matter how many pranks she pulled.

"Khalamoni," Nadia asked as the CNG zoomed past fields and ponds (and maybe some fields that had turned into ponds because of the floodwater, Nadia thought).

"Hmm?" Khalamoni said.

"How do you keep your fasts when you're out working all day?" Nadia asked. She knew if there was anyone who would understand Nadia's struggles, it would be her khalamoni.

"It's not easy," Khalamoni said. "I do the practical things. Make sure I eat a lot at sehri and that I drink a lot of water. And I make sure that even when I'm doing a lot of work, I take breaks and give myself time to rest. And I also get lots of sleep when I can." Khalamoni grinned at Nadia like that should help. But Nadia *had* rested, and she was eating lots of food and drinking plenty of water every sehri, and she *still* found it hard. She hadn't thought fasting would be this difficult.

But then, she had planned to fast during the

summer vacation when there was no school, so she could just relax and not worry too much about anything. She didn't know she would become a serious journalist while fasting!

"It's hard to fast," Nadia said. "I don't know how the people at the shelter do it when I can't!"

"Well . . . Nadia, you're only eight years old," Khalamoni said. Nadia was going to protest—she didn't want to be treated like a kid by her favorite person in the world. But Khalamoni continued before Nadia could say a word, almost like she could read Nadia's mind. "You're very smart and capable, but . . . it's not a *must* for you to fast. And that's for a reason. It's because Allah realizes that not everybody is capable of fasting. Like if you're too sick to fast, or you have a lot of hardship that makes it difficult for you to fast, or if you're still young." At this, Khalamoni gave Nadia a pointed look.

"So why did Jawaria Auntie at the shelter fast?" Nadia asked.

"You'll have to ask her," Khalamoni said with

a shrug. "But . . . maybe fasting makes her feel better. Makes her feel closer to God or gives her peace. Fasting is about a lot more than not eating or drinking, you know."

Nadia nodded like she knew, but she wasn't sure she really understood. Adam had said that fasting was about self-control, and now Khalamoni was saying that fasting was about finding peace and being closer to God. Nadia didn't know what to think. All she knew was that as a journalist, her duty was to ask some more questions and find out a little more about what Ramadan was really about.

Khalamoni's friend arrived at the shelter after them. She showed Khalamoni some photos she had taken of the places that still had floodwater, and the ruined crops and destroyed homes. Then, she started taking pictures of the building and the women in the shelter, while Khalamoni walked around doing more interviews.

Nadia sat down on the steps leading up to the shelter. She was excited for the photo shoot, but some of her excitement had disappeared because of how hot it was. She was surprised when, a few moments later, Reem sat down on the steps next to her.

"You'll get your dress ruined," Nadia said, a little alarmed. Reem was wearing a bright blue-and-yellow salwar kameez with hand-embroidered flowers. Her mom had said in the car that she'd bought it special for Reem's photo shoot.

"That's okay," Reem said. "They're not going to take photos of me from behind."

That was true, Nadia thought, so she scooted over to make more room for Reem. This was the first time the two of them had been alone together, but it didn't feel awkward. They sat in silence for a moment, as Nadia listened to the sounds of the village around them: the wind blowing through the trees, birds singing from somewhere in the distance, and even the sound of rickshaw wheels crunching on the dirt paths.

"Shouldn't you be getting ready for your photos?" Nadia asked after a moment.

Reem sighed, playing with the hem of her dress nervously. "I don't know if I want to take photos."

"Really?" Nadia asked. "But . . . all the best news articles have photos attached to them. And you're so important to Khalamoni's article."

"I know," Reem said. She turned to Nadia with a frown on her face. "I guess I'm nervous to have a photo in a big Western newspaper. When I first started sharing about what happened to our village and about fundraising for our shelter on social media, there were so many people who were annoyed with me because they thought I was too young to take action. What if people read the article and that's all they think about? Maybe your khalamoni shouldn't even talk about me in her article and should focus on the shelter and the women in it instead."

Nadia could tell Reem had been thinking about this a lot. "They'll be in the article too," she said reassuringly, even though she didn't know for sure.

"But your khalamoni said that I'll be the highlight. She said that sometimes people are impressed when young people are speaking up. It shows them that . . . it's a serious issue. But I don't really want to be the highlight. What if it does the opposite of what your khalamoni said and makes people take it less seriously?" Reem asked. "Besides, I didn't do any of this by myself. If it wasn't for my parents, or everyone who helped form this shelter, none of it would have happened. I wish that's what people learned about these floods. One person can't help everyone. It has to be a community. We *all* have to care, and we *all* have to help."

Nadia nodded slowly. What Reem said made sense. It was a big job for one person, even if they wanted to do it all. She wished that Yasmin were here to talk to Reem. Yasmin always knew the right thing to say and how to make someone feel better when they were feeling down. Nadia was better at asking questions and competing. But maybe being a journalist was more than just asking questions to find out the truth. Khalamoni had made sure that Reem and the women in the shelter felt comfortable sharing their experiences with her. If she had just asked the difficult questions, maybe they wouldn't have been so open with her.

Now, it was up to Nadia to make Reem comfortable. To understand where she was coming from, but also to make her understand what Khalamoni wanted to do with her article, and how important it was!

"You're right," Nadia said. "But . . . maybe sometimes one person needs to start things so that other people can learn, right? Like how you saw what happened in your village and it made you want to learn more about climate change. And how your parents said you were the one who came up with the idea for the shelter. And how, even though people were mean to you for being young and trying to do something about the floods, you didn't stop! Everyone was responsible for the shelter, but maybe without you they wouldn't have come together. And I think that's why Khalamoni wants to highlight you . . . because what you did was important!"

Reem smiled. "Maybe you're right. Sometimes one person can make some kind of a difference."

Nadia grinned. "And you definitely taught me a lot of things that I didn't know before I met you."

"Really?"

"Yeah, they don't teach us anything about Bangladesh. We were studying climate change in school this year, and we learned all about renewable energy, and water conservation, and reduce, reuse, recycle. But not about floods in Bangladesh."

"Or the rising sea levels?" Reem asked.

Nadia shook her head.

"The people who get displaced?"

"Nope."

Reem blinked in surprise "They don't teach it to us either. But I thought . . . other places were different. I would have thought they would teach *something.*"

"I wish they did. But that's why Khalamoni wants to do the article properly. Because she cares about what's happening here too. She wants to help. You should talk to her about your worries. She'll understand."

Reem's eyebrows drew together, like she was thinking really hard. "I guess I understand. Maybe if I talk to her, we can really figure out how to make the article right—so it tells people about what's happening here *and* that we're a community helping each other."

"Yes!" Nadia said. She was sure that if anybody could write this article properly, it was her khala-moni.

"Thanks, Nadia. You've been a big help," Reem said, getting up and dusting off her kameez. Then, she reached out a hand toward Nadia. "Want to come watch my photo shoot?"

Nadia took her hand, and Reem pulled her up to stand. The two of them made their way back toward their shelter. Suddenly, Nadia didn't feel so tired anymore. Instead, she felt excited that she could somehow help in telling the story of Reem, the shelter, and all the women here.

Nadia Gets Pranked!

By the time iftar rolled around that evening, Nadia was too tired to function. Her stomach rumbled with hunger, and she was so thirsty she could drink a whole gallon of water!

Finally, the Maghrib call to prayer sounded and Nadia bit into one of the sweet dates Nanu put on her plate and gulped down the water.

"Slow down, Nadia," Ammu said. She sounded a little worried, so Nadia slowed down slightly. She didn't want to give Ammu and Abbu any reasons to suggest she take another break from fasting. She was already behind on the Ramadan race!

"She must be hungry after all the hard work

she's doing," Nanu said with a smile directed at Nadia. She placed more piyajus and shomuchas on Nadia's plate.

"She's not doing work!" Adam said, wrinkling his nose up. "She's just following behind Khalamoni like she always does!"

Khalamoni frowned at Adam. "Adam, that's not very nice. Nadia is helping me loads. Today at the photo shoot, Reem, who is the focus of my feature, was really nervous and I wasn't sure if she would let us take photos of her. But then Nadia talked her into it." Khalamoni glanced at Nadia with a grin, and Nadia felt a warm glow of pride in her chest. She couldn't believe Reem had been thinking of skipping out on the photo shoot altogether, or that *she* had helped make Reem feel more comfortable about doing it.

"I just told her to talk to you!" Nadia said with a grin of her own.

Nadia was excited about her work with Khalamoni and that she was doing things right! She wished that Adam and her cousins could see how she was helping Khalamoni and understood things about the world! But all they cared about was the Ramadan race. Even she couldn't stop thinking about how she was still dead last, especially when Lily and Rosie kept giving her secret looks over their iftar, like they were reminding her that she was going to lose. She had to come up with a plan—and fast.

The next day, Nadia slept in until noon. She stretched her arms and legs and rubbed sleep out of her eyes. She didn't feel too tired.

On the bedside table, there was a glass full of water. And even with the fan running all night, Nadia felt warm and thirsty. She reached over and took a big gulp of water.

And it was only then that she remembered—she was supposed to be fasting!

She heard laughter coming from the doorway and turned to find Adam, Lily, and Rosie giggling.

"You broke your fast, just like we knew you would!" Adam said.

She couldn't believe it—Lily and Rosie had gone behind her back to team up with her brother and prank her!

"You put the glass beside my bed?" Nadia asked.

"It was my idea," Rosie said proudly, standing tall.

"But I was the one who put it there after sehri. I waited until you fell asleep," Adam said with a big, annoying smile.

Nadia's cheeks warmed. She couldn't believe this. She had never come in dead last for anything, and she had never lost like *this*—because her cousins and brother had teamed up to make sure she would lose. She couldn't believe she'd fallen for such a stupid prank. Now she would definitely lose the Ramadan race. She had no hope of catching up when she was two whole fasts behind everyone else!

"I'm telling Ammu!" Nadia said.

She rushed past Adam, Lily, and Rosie in the doorway and ran to find Ammu. She was in the sitting room with a scarf wrapped around her head. She was reading the Qur'an softly, singing the words so they carried in the wind.

"Ammu, Ammu!" Nadia cried.

"What is it, Nadia?" Ammu asked, placing a marker on the page she was reading and glancing up. Her eyebrows were scrunched together like she was worried.

"Adam . . . he . . . he . . . made me break my fast!" Nadia said. She could feel tears pricking the backs of her eyes. But she knew if she started crying, everyone would think she was even more of a baby.

"I didn't!" Adam had followed to the sitting room and stood just behind Nadia. But even from here, Nadia could see that his fingers were crossed behind his back.

"Lying is haram," Nadia said, her voice wavering as she tried to hold back her tears.

"So is being a tattletale," said Adam.

Ammu looked from Nadia to Adam to Lily and Rosie who stood in the doorway, blinking their wide eyes and looking innocent.

"Lily, Rosie . . . did you see what happened?" Ammu asked.

"No, Fufu," they said simultaneously, shaking their heads.

Nadia narrowed her eyes at them. She would get them back.

"Did you make Nadia break her fast?" Ammu asked now, turning to Adam.

"I didn't *make* her," Adam said.

"He *did*!" Nadia cried, stamping her feet on the ground. "He put a glass of water on my bedside table. When I woke up, I forgot I was fasting and that I wasn't supposed to drink any water. So I took a big gulp and now . . . now my fast is broken."

Nadia's voice trembled even more as she explained herself, and before she knew it, she was crying big, fat tears. It was still only the second week of Ramadan, and she was already failing, already falling behind everyone else. Maybe everyone had been right—Nadia couldn't do this. Maybe Nadia was too young.

"Oh, Nadia . . ." Ammu said. She reached her hands and wrapped Nadia up in a hug until she stopped crying. "Just because you accidentally took a gulp of water doesn't mean your fast is broken."

"Really?" Nadia's voice was muffled against Ammu's headscarf.

"Really?" asked Adam, not sounding very happy.

"Really?" asked Lily and Rosie, sounding very interested.

"Really," Ammu said. She pulled out of their hug and wiped away some of Nadia's tears. "You see, Allah sees everything. And he sees your heart."

"My heart?" Nadia asked. Even *she* couldn't see her heart.

"Yes, your heart," Ammu said with a nod. "By that I mean . . . he can see you didn't *mean* to break your fast. He knows your intentions. He knows what you *wanted* to do was to keep your fast. You just had a little accident."

"So . . . I can keep my fast even though I took a drink of water?" Nadia asked.

"Of course, if that's what you want to do." Ammu smiled.

"That's what I want to do," Nadia said, wiping away the tear tracks on her cheeks. Suddenly, she felt a lot better. Ammu always knew how to cheer Nadia up.

"And Adam . . ." Ammu looked at Adam with a frown. Adam tried to look innocent, but everyone here knew that he was guilty. "Allah can see your heart too . . . even if you cross your fingers behind your back."

"So . . . if Allah can see everything, that means he also saw Nadia try to make me break my fast the other day when she tempted me with a box of mishtis!" Adam said.

Now, Ammu turned her frown to Nadia. Nadia wanted to hide away from Ammu's disappointed look, but she had nowhere to hide.

"Nadia, that wasn't a very nice thing to do," Ammu said.

"He got to have mishti afterward," Nadia said. She was sure it wasn't the same thing. Adam had *almost* made Nadia break her fast, but Nadia hadn't even come close to making him break his.

"You both have to stop trying to break each other's fasts," Ammu said. "You should follow your cousins' example. They're not trying to prank each other. They get along." Ammu grinned at Lily and Rosie, who smiled back like they were completely innocent.

"But—" Nadia started.

"It's not very nice to pull pranks, Nadia," Rosie interrupted her before she could finish.

"Tut, tut, Adam," said Lily.

"Now, why don't you both get the Qur'an and we can all read together?" Ammu asked.

"Okay," Nadia and Adam said. Nadia couldn't believe that Rosie and Lily were getting away with their pranking. As she slipped out of the sitting room, she felt more determined than ever to make a comeback in the Ramadan race. She would have to find a way, even if she probably shouldn't try to get anybody to break fasts anymore. But she couldn't let the rest of them win—not after they pulled this prank on her.

NADIA ISLAM'S INVESTIGATIVE QUESTIONS FOR REEM

<u>Question #1</u>: Did Reem worry about being called a baby when she went to her parents to help her village?

<u>Question #2</u>: How did she learn so much about climate change???

<u>Question #3</u>: How can we help Reem with her work?

Nadia Has a Major Fight!

For the next few days, Khalamoni was busy trying to put together her article for the newspaper. Meanwhile, the adults in the house made Nadia, Adam, Lily, and Rosie take more breaks from fasting. Even though they all complained, Nadia was secretly happy about it. She loved fasting during Ramadan and how everyone was doing it together. She loved always breaking her fast at the dinner table surrounded by family after hearing the Maghrib call to prayer from the nearby mosque.

But she also loved having energy to play and run around and think! And on the days when she didn't fast, she made sure to help everyone who *was* fasting in the kitchen because now she knew just how tiring fasting could be, even for adults!

One night after iftar, Nadia borrowed Ammu's tablet so she could have a Zoom call with Yasmin. It had been so long since they had last spoken, and Nadia missed her best friend.

"Hi!" Nadia said as soon as Yasmin's familiar face filled up the screen.

"Hi," said Yasmin, though she sounded more tired than excited. She let out a yawn and blinked her eyes tiredly.

"You're fasting?" Nadia asked.

"Yes, and iftar is hours away," Yasmin complained with a sigh.

"How is your Ramadan going?" Nadia asked. She still wished she could have spent this Ramadan with Yasmin. Maybe Yasmin could have even joined in on the Ramadan race. She wasn't as competitive as Nadia's family—she wasn't really competitive at all. But it would still have been fun to have her best friend by her side.

"It's going okay," Yasmin said. "I keep one fast, and then I take a break. So that helps me get my energy back."

"Really?" Nadia asked. That sounded like a much easier Ramadan than the one Nadia was having. "I've kept ten fasts already!" Since they were halfway through Ramadan, that meant that Nadia had only missed five fasts. She kind of wished she had been able to do Ramadan the way Yasmin had, but there was the Ramadan race to think about!

"Wow!" Yasmin said.

She looked impressed, but Nadia didn't feel like it was impressive at all. "Adam and my cousins have kept eleven, though."

"But they're older than you!" Yasmin said.

"Only by one year," Nadia mumbled. "And now they're winning our race, and I'm losing. Adam even tried to get me to break my fast."

Yasmin blinked at Nadia in shock. "Really?"

"Yes, but . . . I tried to give him sweets to get him

to break his fast first. I teamed up with my cousins to do it and it didn't work. And then Adam tried to get payback by teaming up with them and pranking me with a glass of water on my bedside table. Ammu got annoyed and told us not to break each other's fasts anymore but . . . I have another idea that'll help me win our Ramadan race."

Yasmin didn't look impressed anymore. She sat back with her lips in a thin line. "Nadia . . . this Ramadan race doesn't seem like a good idea. Aren't you supposed to be working on your newspaper article? How will you become editor in chief if you're not concentrating on that?"

"I am, but I've been concentrating on the race too. I need to beat Adam and my cousins," Nadia insisted.

"But Ramadan isn't supposed to be about seeing how many fasts you can keep. My mom told me it was about learning self-control."

That sounded familiar to Nadia. Adam had said the same thing—even if he hadn't been very good at controlling himself when he pranked Nadia.

"She said that during Ramadan, even when we're hungry or thirsty, we make the choice to control ourselves and not eat or drink. It's one of the skills you're supposed to learn as you fast," Yasmin continued.

What Yasmin said made a lot of sense, but it didn't change anything.

"That's not important. Doing the race is making us all better at Ramadan, because we're going to keep more fasts," Nadia replied. She knew that if they weren't doing the Ramadan race, they would probably all keep fewer fasts.

"But Ramadan isn't just about keeping fasts, Nadia," Yasmin said, sounding a little annoyed. "It's also about your intentions. About what you mean to get out of your fast. That's what my dad told me."

Nadia thought about how Ammu had said something similar. She said that Allah could see their hearts. Did that mean Allah could see that in their hearts they were only keeping more fasts to win the Ramadan race?

"It doesn't matter," Nadia told Yasmin, even though she wasn't so sure anymore. "And when I submit my project to Ms. Johnson, she'll see that not only did I do Ramadan and help my aunt, but I also won at Ramadan. I can already see the headline in the school newspaper: Nadia Islam Wins at Ramadan."

Yasmin shook her head slowly with her eyebrows scrunched up. "You can't win at Ramadan. It doesn't work like that."

"But you *can* win a Ramadan race," Nadia said.

Yasmin was silent for a moment. Their video chat felt awkward now. More awkward than it had ever been between Nadia and Yasmin. But Nadia wasn't going to give up the Ramadan race just because Yasmin didn't understand it. She was probably just jealous because Nadia was having fun with her family here while Yasmin was stuck back home doing Ramadan all on her own.

"I'm not sure if I can help you out with the newspaper article anymore, if it's going to be about your Ramadan race," Yasmin mumbled.

"It's not going to be just about Ramadan, but the Ramadan race will be part of it, because it's important!" Nadia insisted. "And it's not fair for you to pull out, just because you don't agree with—"

"I'd rather write my own article about Ramadan instead," Yasmin said. "Because I want to write about what Ramadan is *really* all about. And I'll do my own drawing to go along with it too."

Nadia's stomach sank at Yasmin's words. Nadia was sure that winning the Ramadan race and keeping the most fasts was what was most important. She couldn't believe that Yasmin would write her own article, just because she didn't agree with Nadia.

"Fine, I guess we'll see what Ms. Johnson cares about more!" Nadia said in a huff.

"Fine, Nadia. I'll talk to you later." With that, Yasmin ended the video call.

Nadia felt a swell of tears in her body, but she wasn't going to let a fight with her best friend make her cry. It was just because Nadia and Yasmin were so far away from each other, and because they were both fasting. Ammu and Abbu were always a little bit more irritable when fasting, but in a way, they were a little bit more patient too. If they got annoyed during Ramadan, they would pause and say sorry and try to be better.

Nadia hoped that Yasmin would do the same.

She was sure that in a few days she and Yasmin would be back on good terms again.

For now, she just had to concentrate on winning the Ramadan race.

Nadia's Plans Foiled!

Nadia thought about her fight with Yasmin all night long. She barely got any sleep! She couldn't believe that Yasmin would be so dismissive of the Ramadan race. Why couldn't she understand that everyone here thought Nadia was just a baby and that she *had* to prove them wrong by winning the Ramadan race? Especially now that Adam and her cousins had pranked her. It wasn't fair that she was still dead last after everything!

Nadia was still so annoyed about Yasmin that she tossed and turned all night. When she woke up, it was still dark outside, but she realized that sehri wasn't too far away. Instead of going back to sleep, she washed her face and did wudhu before offering to help the adults by setting the table for sehri.

"You could have rested for a little longer if you wanted, Nadia," Mami said as Nadia carried bowls of rice to the table.

"I know, but I'm not tired!" Nadia said, even though she could feel how heavy her eyelids were from sleep.

"Why don't you go wake up your cousins, Nadia? We can finish setting the table," Mama said.

"Okay, and I'll wake up Adam too," Nadia said.

She walked toward the bedroom she was sharing with Adam. She turned the doorknob and stepped inside. Adam was sound asleep, his chest rising up and down. Nadia already knew Adam was a heavy sleeper. Ammu had to call him multiple times to wake him up. Sometimes even that didn't work; he needed to be shaken awake.

But then she thought about how she was dead last in the Ramadan race, and she wasn't sure if she wanted to shake Adam awake. A plan began to form in her head. One that she was sure would finally help her win the Ramadan race!

"Adam," Nadia said in a whisper, just in case he was awake. He didn't make a sound. He didn't even stir.

Nadia waited a moment before stepping outside the bedroom. She thought about what Ammu had said: that intentions matter when it came to fasting. She hoped that Allah would know that Nadia's intentions were to prove to everyone that she was just as mature as they were. And that she wanted to celebrate her Eid properly. And maybe she also wanted to prove Yasmin wrong about the Ramadan race. Nadia was sure that Allah would understand that. He had to!

Next were Lily and Rosie. Nadia shuffled to their bedroom. She hovered outside this time. She had no idea if Lily and Rosie were heavy or light sleepers. She couldn't risk waking them up by going inside. She waited for just a minute outside the door before turning back toward the dining room.

"They don't want to fast today," Nadia declared once she arrived.

"Are you sure?" Ammu asked. Mama and Mami looked a bit confused too.

"Adam said he was too tired and wanted to take a break," Nadia explained. "And Rosie said she wanted just a day off from fasting, and Lily agreed."

Mama and Mami exchanged a look. "Well, we

have been telling them to take breaks from their fasting. It must be so hard for them in the heat. Lily and Rosie usually keep fewer fasts than they have this year."

Nadia was surprised to hear that. They had acted like keeping so many fasts was no big deal to them. Were they just pretending to impress Nadia and Adam? But Nadia didn't understand why either of them would want to do that.

"Are you sure you don't want to take a break too, Nadia?" Ammu asked. "If you're all taking a break from fasting, you could go out and play together in the morning. And maybe you could get some food to eat from one of the street vendors when they pass by. Some peanuts or coconut water."

"No way!" Nadia said. She hopped onto her chair at the dining table and began to pile chicken sandwiches onto her plate.

Ammu's chicken sandwiches were always delicious, but they tasted weird today. Maybe it was because Nadia felt this pit of guilt in her stomach.

But she was doing the right thing. After this, she wouldn't be dead last anymore. She would finally be on an even playing field.

When Nadia woke up in the morning, she found Adam and her cousins in the sitting room in an angry huddle. They were whispering together, and Nadia was worried that they were whispering about *her*. She didn't know whether to feel worried or happy.

They turned around when Nadia approached, all of them looking very angry with Nadia.

"Why didn't you wake us up this morning?" Rosie asked, stepping forward with her hands on her hips. Rosie was not that much taller than Nadia, but she seemed to tower over her.

"You guys made me almost break my fast with your prank," Nadia said. She wasn't going to back down, even if Rosie was making her a little nervous.

"But we didn't," Adam said. "Ammu said it didn't

count, and so you got to keep your fast."

"Still, you *wanted* to break my fast," Nadia pointed out. "This way, all of us are even. We're all keeping the same number of fasts."

"Uh-uh, no way," Rosie said. She turned to Lily and Adam with a smile on her lips. "We're going to fast today, even if we haven't had sehri."

"We are?" Lily asked.

"Well, I am, because I'm the oldest, and I'm going to win our race. Nadia's silly prank won't beat me." Rosie grinned wider as she turned back to Nadia.

"How can you fast without eating sehri?" Nadia asked. She would have never thought her cousin would suggest something like this.

"I'll just go without eating or drinking until iftar. It's not a big deal," Rosie said.

"Yeah, me too!" Adam chimed in.

"But it'll be so difficult. Won't you be too tired and hungry and thirsty?" Nadia didn't want to think about fasting without eating sehri first.

She got tired and hungry and thirsty even on the days she ate sehri.

"I can do it," said Rosie.

"So can I!" Adam agreed. They both looked at Lily, who didn't seem as enthusiastic about fasting without sehri.

Nadia was hopeful. Maybe it wouldn't be so bad losing the Ramadan race if she and Lily shared the title.

"I can fast without sehri too," she agreed after a moment, and Nadia felt her last chance of success vanish into thin air.

Nadia Needs Advice!

"Do you want to come to a final interview with Reem today?" Khalamoni asked Nadia, peeking into her bedroom later that day. "I had to arrange it last minute because I have some follow-up questions that came up while I was writing my article. Thankfully, Reem and her family are free for a little bit today."

Khalamoni was already dressed and ready to go out in a floral blue salwar kameez. She also had a printed-out draft of the article she had been working on in her hands.

Nadia wanted to go with Khalamoni. She wanted to read Khalamoni's article, but more than that, she wanted to know what Reem thought about it. But Nadia knew that she couldn't. She had to somehow convince Adam, Lily, and Rosie to break their fasts. Otherwise, Nadia would still lose the Ramadan race.

"I can't today. I'm . . . too tired," Nadia said, even though she didn't feel too tired at all. She had eaten a lot at sehri, and it had rained all last night, meaning that there was a breeze coming in through the window.

"Are you sure? I think Reem would really like to see you," Khalamoni said.

Nadia hesitated, feeling her stomach sink with disappointment at the fact that she couldn't go to this interview *and* win the Ramadan race at the same time.

"I'm sure," she said, even though really she wished she could go. Going to these interviews with Khalamoni had been her favorite part of her trip to Bangladesh so far. Sure, she liked hanging out with her cousins, and eating all the delicious food her nanu cooked, but learning about all the work Reem was doing filled Nadia with pride. Even if learning about the floods and climate change also made her sad.

"Okay, Nadia. Have a good day. Rest up," Khalamoni said with a smile. Nadia watched as Khalamoni disappeared from sight. She imagined running behind her and saying that she'd changed her mind! But she knew she couldn't do that.

Throughout the rest of the day, Nadia watched as Adam and her cousins lay in bed or on the couch. Barely moving or talking or doing much at all! They were almost like zombies in the scary movies Nadia wasn't supposed to watch.

Nadia knew she wanted to convince them to break their fasts, but as she watched them she felt more guilty than determined. She was the reason Adam and her cousins were suffering. Nadia's guilt got bigger and bigger in her stomach. It felt even bigger than her hunger or her thirst. She wasn't sure what she was supposed to do.

"Do you guys want to play some ludo?" Nadia

asked the three of them in the sitting room.

"No," Rosie groaned. "I'm too tired."

"Do you guys want to go out and get some food for iftar?" Nadia asked.

"No, I'm too hungry to go out," said Adam.

"Do you want to read the Qur'an together to help pass the time before iftar?" Nadia asked.

"No, I'm too thirsty to read the Qur'an," said Lily in a small voice.

The three of them slouched back on the couch, looking very unlike the brother and cousins Nadia knew.

"Looks like a hard day of fasting," Nanu said as she peeked through the sitting room door.

Lily, Adam, and Rosie groaned in response, while Nadia's guilt grew so big she felt like she couldn't keep it in anymore. She had to find a way to make everything better.

She left the sitting room to find her ammu.

Ammu was on her bed, reading the Qur'an once more, her lips moving to the words of the surah she was reading but making no sound.

"Ammu . . ." Nadia said.

She looked up from the Qur'an, her eyebrows threaded together with surprise. "Nadia! I thought you would have gone out with your khalamoni today?"

"No, I decided I didn't want to because . . . because I did something bad," Nadia said. She looked down at the carpet of the bedroom instead of at Ammu.

Ammu sighed. "Even though we talked a few days ago, and I told you that Allah can always see your heart?"

"Yes . . . I'm sorry," Nadia said. "I didn't wake up Adam or Lily or Rosie for sehri this morning on purpose. I only pretended to wake them up. None of them told me they didn't want to fast. And now, they're keeping their fasts even though they didn't eat sehri. They're tired and hungry and thirsty. They don't want to play with me or go out or read the Qur'an together or do anything!"

"Oh no . . ." Ammu said. "Nadia, why would you do something like that?"

"I just want to win our Ramadan race," Nadia confessed. When she finally looked up at Ammu, she didn't look confused anymore. She looked angry with her lips in a thin line.

"Your Ramadan race?" she asked.

Nadia's stomach sank when she realized what she had accidentally let slip. "We wanted to see who could keep the most fasts this year. Lily and Rosie said they could keep them all and so did Adam, and I didn't want to be the loser. And then I had to break my fast because I was helping Khalamoni, so I *was* a loser. I had to do something to win!"

As she heard the words she was saying, Nadia realized that she had made a big mistake. She wasn't just losing the Ramadan race; she was also losing at being a good Muslim. Nadia thought maybe her intention to prove to everyone that she wasn't just a baby was important enough that she could pull her prank. But it didn't matter. She could have done something good instead today, like helping Khalamoni or learning more about climate change from Reem. Instead, she had tried to make her brother and cousins break their fasts, and Allah had seen it all. Ammu had said that Allah saw everything. So he saw her pretend to wake up Adam and her cousins. He saw her lying to Ammu and even to Khalamoni. He saw her being a bad sister and a bad cousin.

"Nadia. . . ." Ammu sighed again. "You know that Ramadan isn't about racing to keep the most fasts, right?"

"I know. . . ." Nadia said. Yasmin had tried to explain it to her, but Nadia hadn't listened. "It's about learning self-control and having the intention to fast."

Ammu finally smiled, and Nadia felt a little better. Maybe she wasn't the worst Muslim in the world.

"Yes, it is a little about that. But it's about a lot

more than that. It's about feeling close to Allah. It's about being generous and about community. Like what your friend Reem is doing. She's been generous with her time, with her actions. She's been helping rebuild her community when it's been hit hard by the floods."

Nadia realized that Ammu was right. Back home, Nadia and her family always did a lot more than fasting during Ramadan. They shared food with friends and family and even with people at their mosque. And Ammu would always sit with her and Adam so they could read the Qur'an together. All of that made her feel closer to Allah, and it made her feel closer to her community.

The Ramadan race didn't make her feel any of those things.

"We have to do something, Ammu. We have to get Adam, Lily, and Rosie to break their fasts!" Nadia said. They were suffering because of her, and she had to find a way to make things right.

"I can try to talk to them, but if their intention

is to fast, they might not be convinced so easily," Ammu said.

"But it's my fault that they didn't get to have sehri," Nadia said. She wished that she was the one suffering today instead of them. Even if they had tried to pull a prank on her.

"I have an idea!" Nadia knew how she could make things at least a little bit better.

CHAPTER 22

Nadia Makes a Grand Apology!

Nadia explained her plans to all the adults in the house. She even called Khalamoni to tell her everything. Everyone wanted to help Nadia.

Nadia began to work. She wasn't so good at cooking, but back home Nadia liked helping Ammu in the kitchen and it wasn't so different from helping Nanu here. She just had to remember her Bengali words.

Nadia passed Nanu whatever she asked for in the kitchen. She stirred the pot when Nanu told her to. She chopped up some fruits and vegetables. She even helped Nanu fold some pasties.

"Come on, guys, it's almost time for iftar!" Nadia said, running into the sitting room.

Adam, Lily, and Rosie all groaned but they got up from the couch. They did wudhu, and Nadia and her cousins wrapped scarves around their heads while Adam put a tupi on his.

They went into the kitchen, and Nadia watched as Adam and her two cousins stared in surprise at the dinner table.

"We're having a big Ramadan feast full of your favorite foods!" Nadia announced.

"Wow!" Rosie said, her eyes wide.

Adam sat down on his chair, like he was ready to dive into his meal, while Lily sat down and stared at each food item, like she was taking everything in slowly.

"We all worked together to make your favorite Ramadan foods: haleem and piyajus for Adam, aloo chop and beguni for Rosie, and khichuri with chicken curry for Lily. Khalamoni even brought fresh fruits from the shop: mangoes, guavas, oranges, boroi, and lychee," Nadia explained. Mama and Mami had told Nadia these were some

of Lily and Rosie's favorite fruits.

They all sat down at the table and said a prayer before Maghrib azan. When the call to prayer began, everyone broke their fasts together with dates.

Adam spooned haleem into a bowl while Rosie piled her plate with aloo chop and beguni and Lily mixed khichuri with chicken curry. They all tasted a bit of everything alongside their favorite foods—everyone did.

"This is delicious!" Rosie declared. Adam and Lily nodded in agreement.

Nadia began to eat too, but she knew that she hadn't made things quite right yet.

"Adam, Rosie, Lily . . . I'm sorry I didn't wake you up for sehri today," she said. "And I'm sorry I lied to you about it, Ammu and Mami. And I'm sorry I lied to you, Khalamoni, and said that I was too tired to help today."

Adam, Rosie, and Lily exchanged glances between them. Nadia waited, hoping that they would be willing to forgive and forget.

"It's okay," Adam said with a shrug. "It was kind of a clever prank. I guess we have to give you credit for that."

"And we'll get you back," Rosie said, puffing out her chest like she was very determined.

Nadia took a deep breath and said, "Well, I'm not doing the Ramadan race anymore. So . . . you don't have to get me back."

Across the table, Ammu beamed at Nadia with

pride. Nadia felt a swell of pride too, in her chest, even if she felt a little embarrassed to admit all of this out loud to everyone in her family.

"What?" Rosie asked, her look of determination suddenly replaced with a glare. "Really? Just because your silly plan didn't succeed you want to drop out?"

"I don't want to do it anymore either," Lily said quietly. Rosie turned sharply toward her sister.

"Lily!" she said.

"I'm sorry, but it's not fun to pull pranks on each other and try to break each other's fasts," Lily said. "Ramadan was way more fun before, when we fasted and read Qur'an together and gave iftar to all our neighbors. Remember how last year you and I learned how to make aloo chop so we could give it to the family next door? We haven't done any of that this year."

Nadia was surprised that she and Lily were on the same page for once. But it made her feel brave enough to continue.

"I agree with Lily!" she declared. "It's my first Ramadan fasting, and I'm not having any fun. And I don't feel closer to Allah, or even to my own brother or cousins. Ammu told me that Ramadan was about being generous and about community."

But Rosie crossed her arms over her chest and frowned at Nadia. "Whatever, you guys all lose the race, I guess."

"Rosie." Mami tutted. "You're the eldest cousin; you should understand where Nadia is coming from. She's right—Ramadan is about a lot more than just keeping fasts, and it's not about winning or losing or one-upping one another."

Mama nodded along too, and Nadia felt reassured.

Rosie still didn't look happy, but Nadia knew the matter was concluded. There would be no more Ramadan races, at least not any that involved Nadia.

* * *

As Nadia prepared for bed that night, she wondered how long Adam and Rosie would be mad at her and Lily for not wanting to do the Ramadan race anymore. She left the bathroom and went to the bedroom she was sharing with Adam. He was already lying down, but in her spot on the bed this time!

"Why are you sleeping on my side of the bed?" Nadia asked. She wondered if this was Adam's way of getting back at Nadia!

Adam looked up at her, and his eyes seemed heavy with sleep already.

"I thought you wanted the side by the window," Adam grumbled. "I can move back, if you don't want it anymore."

Nadia couldn't believe it. Adam was giving her his side of the bed. The side that got the nice, pleasant breeze from the window.

"You're really giving me your side of the bed?" Nadia asked, narrowing her eyes. She was suspicious about Adam's sudden act of kindness—

especially after the prank she had pulled!

"Yes! I've had it all summer, so now you can have it for a little bit," Adam said. "But if you don't want it then—"

"No, I want it!" Nadia interrupted, jumping into bed beside Adam and lying down. She gave Adam a big grin, and Adam returned it. Nadia wondered if this was Adam's way of saying that he wasn't mad at Nadia about the Ramadan race. Sometimes, Adam could be an amazing big brother.

The Spirit of Ramadan

Nadia was ready to start Ramadan fresh with all the new things that she had learned about it. She would practice self-control, and whatever she did would be with good intentions. Nadia knew she still had to make up with Yasmin, but she wasn't sure exactly how to apologize yet, so that would have to wait. She decided that she wouldn't fast the next day so she could be ready and able to help Khalamoni with whatever was left of the article.

In the morning, Nadia woke up feeling refreshed. She knocked on the door of Nanu's bedroom, where Khalamoni had been sleeping too.

"Nadia," Khalamoni said when she opened the

door. Khalamoni didn't look excited at all. She had red eyes, and her long black hair was messy. She looked like she hadn't slept all night long.

"Khalamoni, are you okay?" Nadia asked, concerned.

"I'm fine. Just . . . a little tired. I was up late working on the article," Khalamoni said, rubbing her eyes and smoothing down her hair.

"I can help you today with your article," Nadia said. She hoped that she wasn't too late, and Khalamoni hadn't already finished everything! "I'm ready and I'm going to give it my one hundred percent!"

Khalamoni smiled, but even her smile looked tired. "That sounds great, Nadia. But . . . I have a meeting with the newspaper where I pitched the article today, which I need to focus on."

"Oh." Nadia's excitement deflated like a balloon.

"Sorry, Nadia. Maybe later."

With that, Khalamoni closed the bedroom door with a click.

Nadia hoped she hadn't missed her chance to do something good this Ramadan. Being able to shadow Khalamoni while she interviewed Reem, her family, and the women at the shelter had been amazing. It had been in the spirit of Ramadan. But maybe Nadia had messed it all up by being too focused on the silly Ramadan race.

On the other side of the door, Nadia heard the sound of Khalamoni's computer being switched on. It was such an old laptop that it made a loud *whoosh* when it turned on. Nadia knew she should leave and go back to her room, maybe even find Adam or her cousins so that they could play together. But . . . she wanted to know more about Khalamoni's article. She wanted to help. So instead, she kneeled outside Khalamoni's door, holding her breath and listening as Khalamoni began her meeting.

She hoped that Allah would understand she was eavesdropping for a good reason, not for a bad one.

Nadia listened as Khalamoni exchanged greetings with the people from the newspaper, but there was something wrong. She could tell from the tone of the conversation. It sounded too serious.

"So, did you have a chance to read the article?" Khalamoni asked. "I'm open to suggestions, but I thought this latest draft was pretty good, and Reem approved it too."

"It was good, very good," a man, who Nadia was sure had to be in charge, said.

"Oh, great." Khalamoni sounded relieved as she spoke. "You didn't send any notes, so I was worried that it needed a huge rewrite. So, when do you think the piece will run? I think the sooner the better since things here are still—"

"We actually can't run the piece," the man said, interrupting Khalamoni.

Nadia leaned closer to the door, pressing her ear against the wood. They couldn't run it? What did that mean?

"Okay, if not . . . soon, maybe in a few weeks? Next month? End of summer? It wouldn't be ideal, but . . ." Khalamoni trailed off.

"Well, we thought that we would have space for it originally, but it just doesn't seem possible anymore," the man said.

But what about all the work Khalamoni had been doing? What about Reem? What about the women in the shelter? Nadia wanted to burst in through the door and tell the man how important this was. Maybe he just didn't understand because he wasn't here. He hadn't spoken to Reem or the women in the shelter.

"I don't understand. You said that you wanted pieces specifically about climate change, and when you accepted my piece you said that it was exactly what you were looking for," Khalamoni said. Her voice was calm, but Nadia could hear the angry undertone to it. It wasn't a tone she had heard Khalamoni use before. "The work that Reem is doing here is really important. And ever since monsoon season started, things have been getting even worse. This article could help people. Not just raise awareness, but with immediate action too. It could direct people to donate money, which is really necessary right now."

There was that word: *monsoon*. Nadia couldn't imagine things getting worse when they had already been so bad.

"I'm sorry, but there are climate change protests happening in France and that's obviously more relevant. Things have erupted here last week, and that's what we need to cover for now. We won't have space for another climate change feature alongside that," the man said, and Nadia thought he didn't sound sorry at all.

"But this is just as important as what's happening in France. Maybe there's a way the stories can even work together. Two sides of—"

"I'm sorry, we have to kill the article," the man said, interrupting Khalamoni. "You'll obviously still get a fee for all the work that you did, which we appreciate."

"Yeah, thanks," Khalamoni said so quietly that Nadia could barely hear her. This was another tone Nadia had never heard her khalamoni use: defeated.

"Your writing is great, and we'd love to see a pitch from you again. This one just didn't work out," the man said.

"Sure, I'll make sure to pitch you again," Khalamoni said in her defeated voice. Nadia heard the click of the laptop being shut. Khalamoni didn't come out of the bedroom.

Nadia hovered outside for a minute, feeling frozen with sadness. Finally, she turned and walked toward the sitting room.

Adam and Lily were playing a video game together on Lily and Rosie's gaming console. Rosie sat on the couch, watching with pursed lips. She was still annoyed that Nadia had told everyone about the Ramadan race and that it had ended. But Nadia didn't care about that right now.

She sat down on the couch next to Rosie, feeling just as defeated as Khalamoni had sounded. She watched the racing cars of Adam and Lily's game, and usually she would be jumping to join in. But today, she didn't want to play any games.

"What's wrong, Nadia?" Lily asked after a moment when their race had ended and Lily had won.

"You want to play? I bet I can beat you," Adam said.

"She'd have to beat *me*, since I'm the reigning champion," Lily said.

Nadia shook her head. "I don't want to play."

"Probably for the same reason Nadia gave up on the Ramadan race. Because she's a sore loser," Rosie said with her arms crossed.

"There are more important things than winning!" Nadia said finally. She was tired of Rosie being angry at her about something as silly as the Ramadan race. "Like the article Khalamoni was working on, but now the newspaper canceled it so it's never going to get published." Nadia's eyes filled with tears, but she blinked them away. If this was how she was feeling, she couldn't imagine how bad Khalamoni had felt. She had spent all this time working away, only for it all to go to waste. Nadia didn't even want to think about Reem. How would she feel when Khalamoni told her?

"They canceled her article?" Lily asked. She looked at Nadia with concern in her eyes.

"Yes, at least that's what I heard the newspaper

man telling her in their meeting. I wasn't supposed to listen, but I couldn't help it. Now all our hard work is going to go to waste, and nobody outside of Bangladesh will know about the floods or about the climate change here. They'll keep thinking it's all about reduce, reuse, recycle!" Nadia said.

Adam and her cousins only blinked at her. Nadia felt like this entire summer had been for nothing. She had thought that she couldn't afford to lose the Ramadan race, but now Nadia was losing so much more, and so were people that she cared about.

"So what does that mean for the girl that Khalamoni was interviewing?" Adam asked. This was the most he had asked about Khalamoni's work during their entire time in Bangladesh. Nadia couldn't be annoyed with him—she had never really tried to tell Adam about it either.

"I don't know. Khalamoni hasn't told her yet," Nadia said.

"And she's been really helping people, hasn't she?" Lily asked quietly.

Nadia nodded. "She helped people who lost everything during the floods. Her family built this shelter that's on higher ground so that they have a safe place to stay. She was raising money to help them even more. She was helping them find jobs so that they could get back on their feet. She was doing more than anybody I've ever met, and she wasn't even asking for anything in return."

"Can't you do something about it?" Adam asked. "You're a journalist too."

Hearing Adam call Nadia a journalist was weird because Adam always saw Nadia as a baby.

"But . . . I'm *not* a journalist," Nadia said. "I only write down facts and the things that I learn. I haven't even had an article published in my school newspaper yet."

"What are you going to write for your school newspaper?" Lily asked.

"I was going to write about everything I learned in Bangladesh. It was going to be about the Ramadan race, and Reem, and climate change. But now . . . I don't know if I want to write anything!" Nadia said.

"You have to write!" Lily said. "At least if you write about it, someone will know. Even if it's not in a big newspaper."

Adam nodded in agreement. "Maybe Ms. Johnson will even put it on the front page. It can still be an article. People can still learn!"

Nadia guessed that was true, but it didn't fill her up with happiness like it might have at one time. She liked that she would be doing this for school, and of course she wanted to be on the front page of the school newspaper. But none of it seemed fair. Reem should be on the front page of a big newspaper, one that was read across the country—across the whole world! And so should the news about what was happening in Bangladesh. From the floods in Sylhet to the coastal land going underwater with time. From the women in Reem's shelter to everyone displaced on the coasts. It was all part of the same story, and it deserved to be heard.

Nadia realized that Khalamoni had been right about how sometimes big newspapers didn't care about the facts or about telling everyone's stories.

"Maybe if it's really good . . ." Nadia mumbled.

Adam and Lily nodded, but Nadia was sure they knew it wasn't the same thing at all.

They went back to their video game quietly, even though the air felt defeated in the same way Nadia was.

Nadia Is Stuck!

After iftar that day, Nadia opened up her sparkly purple notebook. She took out her pen, ready to write . . . but for once, no words came! All her words felt stuck in her brain, jumbled together. Nadia knew it was because of the conversation she had overheard in Khalamoni's bedroom. Khalamoni had seemed sad the entire day, even as they all broke fast with dates and glasses of freshly squeezed lemonade that Nanu made special for all of them.

Nadia couldn't write about what she was learning in Bangladesh when suddenly everything felt pointless. Nadia had always thought being a journalist meant having the ability to speak up and use your voice to help people. She saw the way Khalamoni used her journalism to shine a light on different people's stories. But now she couldn't even shine a light on someone from her own community. It made Nadia's heart feel heavy. How could she think about writing for a big newspaper like *The New York Times* in the future, when those papers didn't seem to care about stories of people like Reem?

"Nadia?" Khalamoni was at the door, and her voice interrupted Nadia's thoughts. "Are you busy writing?"

Nadia shook her head. "My words are stuck."

"Ah, that happens to me sometimes too."

"Really?" Nadia asked.

"Yeah, I think it happens to everyone. Writing isn't always easy. And sometimes writing about real-life things can be difficult," Khalamoni said with a smile. "What are you writing about? Maybe I can help?"

Nadia wasn't sure if she could, but Khalamoni

was the one person who would understand. "Well, I've been writing about all of the things I've learned in my time in Bangladesh. Like I wrote about how long the flight was, and all the delicious food, and the way Sylhet looks from the inside of Mama's car, and the Ramadan race, and how Rosie got angry when I didn't want to do it anymore. And I wrote all about Reem and the things she taught me about climate change, and the floods, and all the people who are getting . . . displaced. But . . ." Nadia sighed. "But then I overheard your conversation."

Khalamoni sighed too, and there was sympathy in her eyes. She walked over and sat down on the bed beside Nadia.

"I think it's really great that you've been writing about all of the things you've learned. And you shouldn't let a setback stop you from writing more."

"You're not mad that I listened to your conversation?" Nadia asked.

"No, I had a feeling you might," Khalamoni said

with a grin. "When I was your age, I would have definitely listened in on the conversation."

"Aren't you sad that your article won't be published? You worked so hard on it. It's not fair. . . ."

Khalamoni sighed again. "Nadia, if you want to be a journalist, that's one of the things you have to learn. Things aren't always fair. It's really unfair that the newspaper wants to cover protests in France but not what's happening here in Bangladesh. It's unfair that I worked hard for an article that won't get published. It's unfair that Reem thought she would have a chance to spread awareness about her work here, but now we'll have to break the news to her that it won't happen."

But Nadia didn't want to learn about unfair things. If being a journalist meant things would always seem so unfair, she wasn't sure if she wanted to be a journalist.

"What's the point of being a journalist then?" she asked, her arms crossed.

Khalamoni chuckled. "Well, sometimes things

are fair. All of the stories I've covered that you've loved reading. If I didn't research and write them, maybe those people's stories would have never been heard in the way they have been. There are both good and bad parts to being a journalist."

"I wish it was all good parts," Nadia mumbled.

"Me too," Khalamoni said. "But what you write about the summer can still be one of the good parts. You can still share it with your classmates and in your school newspaper. That's important too."

"I guess," Nadia said. She felt a little better because of Khalamoni's words. Nadia had thought that being a journalist was all about asking difficult questions, finding out the truth, and writing down what you found. She had never considered that someone had to print what you wrote too; and that might not always happen.

She opened her notebook and quickly wrote down her new inspiration about journalism!

25

Reem Finds Out the Bad News!

Khalamoni invited Reem and her family over for iftar a few days later, which meant that everybody was buzzing around the house all day preparing. Nanu and Ammu were in the kitchen, making enough food to feed the entire family. Everyone else, including Nadia, cleaned the house top to bottom. Even Rosie, who had been avoiding Nadia since the Ramadan race had been called off, had to help clean. The whole evening was a group effort.

Nadia didn't like doing chores, but as she set the table with an annoying Adam by her side, she decided she didn't mind them so much when she had her entire family to share them with. It was a lot of family, but she liked that. It made sharing everything a lot more fun. She just wished that Yasmin was here too, to share with her and her family. But the thought of Yasmin made Nadia's stomach ache with guilt. The two of them were still in a fight, and Nadia had been too caught up in the Ramadan race and Reem to tell Yasmin that she had been right all along!

Finally, a few hours before iftar, the doorbell rang. Nadia ran up to the door and flung it open. She had been waiting for so long to introduce Reem to her family that even the idea of breaking the bad news to Reem couldn't overshadow her excitement. Reem and her parents stood at the door, wearing much fancier clothes than Nadia had ever seen them in. Reem wore a pastel pink salwar kameez with jewels dotting the hemline, her mom wore a sky-blue saree, and her dad wore a white panjabi with matching sky-blue accents.

"Assalam alaikum, Nadia," Reem said with a grin.

"Walaikum salam!" said Nadia. "Come in!" She led them inside and toward the sitting room, where everyone else was waiting.

"This is my whole family!" Nadia said as an introduction. "And this is Reem!"

Khalamoni made proper introductions of everyone after saying salaam.

"Your house is beautiful," Asifa Auntie said, though she looked between all the adults as she said it like she wasn't sure who the compliment should be paid to.

"Thank you," Nanu said with a smile, which Reem's parents returned.

"And thank you for having us over for iftar. You really didn't have to," Reyhan Uncle said.

"It was the least that we could do," Khalamoni said.

"Besides, Nadia has been talking our ears off about Reem and the article her khalamoni is writing," Ammu said, ruffling Nadia's hair teasingly.

Nadia gave her a mock glare, but inside she was beaming. She was glad that Reem had gotten the chance to meet everyone and everyone had gotten a chance to meet Reem. Even if it was a little bit of a sad occasion.

"I do have some news to share," Khalamoni said after a beat of silence. Her voice was somber. Nadia felt a sinking in her stomach. She had hoped that Khalamoni would share the news at the very end—so they could enjoy their iftar together. "It's about the article."

"Oh," Reem said, glancing at Khalamoni with a curious expression. "You changed it?"

"No, not exactly," Khalamoni said. "It's just . . . I had a meeting with some of the people from the newspaper that I pitched the article to the other day, and it seems there's been some more pressing news to cover elsewhere. They don't have space for it in the newspaper anymore. They're killing it."

"Ah," Reem said. She nodded but didn't say any more. She didn't even seem sad about it, really.

"I'm sorry. I know we all put a lot of work into it. You spent so long answering my questions, having your picture taken. And everybody at the shelter was so generous with their time. . . ." Khalamoni said, her words heavy.

"It's okay, I understand," Reem said. And she sounded like she really did understand.

"Aren't you sad?" Nadia couldn't help but blurt out. "I mean . . . nobody will know now about the shelter or the floods or . . . or . . . anything!"

Reem shrugged. "I guess I'm a little sad, but . . . it's not true that nobody will know. You all know, and you didn't before, right?"

Nadia nodded, and so did everyone else. Especially Adam, who nodded so hard he looked like a bobblehead.

"It would have been nice if more people knew, but none of it changes much for us, I think." Reem looked to her parents, as if for approval, and they both nodded too. "We do the work because somebody has to. We do it for our community, and for all of the people who need the help. If the article got published and more people knew, that would be great, and it would have helped us. But article or no article, we will keep doing the work that we do."

Nadia hadn't really thought about it like that. Reem was right: She and her family had been doing this long before Khalamoni came along to write about it, and she would probably do it for long after. She didn't do it so people abroad would listen or care. She did it because *she* cared about the people here who needed help.

"I guess you're right," Nadia said. "And at least for now, maybe we can help you do what you do."

Reem grinned at Nadia. "Maybe you can!"

Yasmin Comes Up with an Idea!

Nadia may have fixed everything with the Ramadan race, but she and Yasmin were still in a fight. At least, that's what she thought. It was difficult to know when they weren't in the same city. Not even in the same country!

Usually, when Nadia and Yasmin were fighting, they would ignore each other for a few hours. But they couldn't ignore each other for much longer than that. They still had to sit beside each other in school, and Ms. Johnson always gave them group work which meant Nadia and Yasmin had to work together. After a few hours, one of them would always cave and say sorry. And the other would say sorry too, even if she didn't think she was completely in the wrong.

Nadia knew that's just how friendships were. Except this time Nadia knew she was completely in the wrong and Yasmin had been right all along. And they had gone without speaking for days, not just hours.

Nadia knew she had a lot to make up for, but making up started with breaking the silence between them. She had been so worried about Khalamoni's article and Reem that she hadn't had the chance to talk to Yasmin yet. But she finally felt ready to apologize properly, so she made a call to Yasmin, hoping she wasn't too upset with Nadia to answer.

Yasmin answered after a few rings.

"Hi, Nadia," she said. She didn't sound very happy about speaking to Nadia.

"Hi, Yasmin. . . ." Nadia said. She didn't know how to begin with her apology, but at least they were speaking. There was silence for a moment, and Nadia hated having awkward silences in her conversations with Yasmin. They were supposed to be best friends. They should be able to share anything with each other. They should definitely be able to make up from a silly fight with no problems.

"I wish you were here. It's difficult when you're so far away," Nadia blurted out.

Yasmin was quiet for a moment. "Yeah, it *is* difficult when we're so far away from each other. And when it's Ramadan and we're fasting. Sometimes, I get really hungry and cranky. Or really hungry and tired."

"Me too," Nadia said. "Or really hungry and . . . my brain is all jumbled up like puzzle pieces!"

"And it feels like there are missing pieces!" Yasmin adds.

"Exactly." Nadia was glad she and Yasmin were on the same page, at least. "But . . . I'm sorry that I wasn't listening when you told me that the Ramadan race wasn't a good idea. You were right all along."

"I'm sorry too. I probably shouldn't have said that I would just write my own article because we didn't agree. We could have figured something out instead of fighting about it," Yasmin said.

"So, can we work together again? Because things are not going well here!" Nadia said. She filled Yasmin in on everything that had happened with the end of the Ramadan race, the article being cancelled, and Reem's response to it all. "So now our only way to get the word out is through *our* article. If Ms. Johnson really likes it and puts it on the front page of the school newspaper, at least everyone in our school will know."

"Hmm . . ." Yasmin said. "Maybe there's more we can do. I mean, journalism is about reporting the news, right? It doesn't matter if it's an article or . . . something else."

"I guess," Nadia said.

"So, what if you find a way to *show* everyone what's happening in Bangladesh?" Yasmin asked. "You can be like a reporter on a news channel.

You and your khalamoni can interview Reem in a video and even show everyone the shelter. It'll be like . . . like they're taking your trip to Bangladesh with you!"

Nadia couldn't believe she hadn't thought about that herself. "And we can post it online so anybody in the world could watch it."

"Yes!" Yasmin said.

"And you'll help?" Nadia asked.

"Duh!" said Yasmin, like the two of them had never been in a fight at all. This was why Nadia loved her best friend.

NADIA ISLAM'S FACTS ABOUT JOURNALISM

#1: Journalism can be done through lots of different mediums like newspapers, radio, TV, and even the internet.

#2: There are lots of different types of journalists. Some journalists report the news with facts and figures, some might write only about celebrities, and some might just share their opinions.

#3: Journalism is really important! Sometimes, we only know about something that has happened because journalists reported the news on it.

#4: Even though journalism is important, not everyone's stories get told and that's not good. Like how the newspaper Khalamoni pitched Reem's story to thought it was more important to talk about climate change protests in France than floods in Bangladesh.

#5: You don't have to work for a big newspaper in order to be a journalist. You can be a freelancer like Khalamoni or maybe you can even record your own interview and report and upload it online like me and my family!

Nadia Recruits Help

Once Nadia got off the phone with Yasmin, she knew she had a lot of work to do. First, she went to Khalamoni. When she told her the idea Yasmin had come up with, Khalamoni's eyes lit up.

"Nadia, that's brilliant!" she said. "And I've already got a draft of the article I was writing. We can use it to figure out how to direct the video. Which parts of Reem's story, and the shelter's story, are the most important."

"And maybe we can even put some of the important parts in the video. Like the . . . numbers!" Nadia said.

Khalamoni chuckled. "Yes, the overall statistics

and percentages will be very important to put in." She paused and drew her eyebrows together, like she was thinking very hard. "But Nadia, I'm not sure how we'll pull this off. We're not exactly a news crew."

"We can ask everyone to help," Nadia said. "They helped with the iftar feast."

Khalamoni sighed. "They did. But making an iftar feast is a little easier than filming a news segment."

"But we're a lot of people!" Nadia insisted. "There's me and Adam. Lily and . . . maybe Rosie will help. Ammu and Abbu. Mama and Mami. Nanu. Reem, her parents." Nadia ticked everyone off on her fingers. It felt like enough people to Nadia. "And my best friend Yasmin said she'll help too in whatever way she can!"

Khalamoni nodded, though she still didn't look convinced. "How about you ask your brother and cousins and I'll ask everyone else?"

Nadia wasn't so sure if she could convince Rosie

to help, but she didn't want Khalamoni to be even more doubtful of her plans. So she said, "Okay!" in the most confident voice she had.

Adam was lying down in the bedroom, reading a book. He didn't even notice when Nadia barged inside.

"Adam?" she asked.

"Hmm?" Adam said, not looking up.

"Do you want to help Khalamoni and me with getting the word out about Reem and the shelter?" Nadia asked.

Adam put down his book and sat up in bed. "How?"

"Well, Yasmin and I came up with an idea. But we'll need everyone's help if we want to do it right."

Adam looked thoughtful for a moment. Nadia was worried that he might say no. After all, Nadia and Adam didn't always get along and Adam didn't always want to do things that helped Nadia.

But then he shrugged and said, "Okay," before

going back to reading his book.

Nadia grinned. She wanted to throw her arms around her brother and say thank you, but she didn't. That might be a bit weird. Adam could be annoying, but sometimes, like today, she was glad that she had a brother like him.

Next, Nadia approached Lily and Rosie's bedroom. Nadia gulped, worried about what her cousins might say. It had been easy to convince Adam—he had barely even asked any questions. But Lily and Rosie might be more difficult. Still, she knocked loudly on the door.

"Come in!" said Lily at the same time that Rosie asked, "Who is it?"

Nadia wasn't sure what to do. She stood there for a moment and then said, "It's Nadia!"

"Come inside!" Lily called again, so Nadia pushed the door open. Lily and Rosie were each at their respective desks on either side of the room. Rosie had her headphones half on and half off, and Lily was drawing something in a sketchbook.

"What is it?" Rosie asked, not looking very happy to see Nadia.

"Well . . . I was wondering if you wanted to help Reem tell the world her story," Nadia said.

"You want help writing your article for the school newspaper?" Lily asked.

"No . . . my friend Yasmin and I had another idea, and Khalamoni said we need *everyone's* help to do it," Nadia said.

"What's the idea?" Rosie asked.

"We're going to make a video and show everyone the shelter and the floods. And we're going to interview Reem so she can tell people about her work. And then we're going to put it online so everyone can see it. It won't be the same as being in a newspaper, but it might still be good," Nadia said.

"I want to help!" Lily chimed in. They both looked at Rosie, who was silent.

"It's not going to be easy to make a good video," Rosie finally said.

"I know. . . ." Nadia replied.

"And you can't just film it on a phone," Rosie said.

"Why not?" Nadia asked. She didn't think they had the money to buy a fancy video camera.

"Because it'll look unprofessional," Rosie said. "My friend's mom is a videographer. That means someone who makes videos. She's really good. I can ask my friend if her mom can help."

"Really?" Nadia couldn't believe it. Not only was Rosie on board with the project, but she was helping in more ways than Nadia could have imagined.

"I guess." Rosie shrugged. "I mean, it's important for people to know about this. And it's a good idea, making the video."

"Thanks, Rosie," Nadia said.

Rosie shrugged again. Nadia turned around and was about to slip out the door but Rosie's voice stopped her.

"Nadia . . ." Rosie called.

She turned around again.

"You were right to stop the Ramadan race. And I guess about . . . what Ramadan is really about."

Nadia couldn't believe Rosie had admitted that she was wrong!

"But . . . I still would have won *if* we were doing it," Rosie said with a grin.

Nadia grinned too. "Maybe," she said. Nadia guessed being a little competitive was something all the Islams had in common. And maybe that wasn't the worst thing in the world.

CHAPTER 28

Nadia Becomes an Interviewer!

With everyone on board, the plans came together like magic. Nadia could hardly believe it.

Rosie's friend's mom agreed to use her camera equipment to film everything. Nanu, Ammu, and Abbu offered to make food for everyone, so that they had enough energy. Mama and Mami said they'd drive people to and from the shelter, or Reem's village, or anywhere else they needed to go, since they knew the roads of Sylhet best. Rosie and Lily would work on hair, makeup, and wardrobe—they said they knew exactly how everyone should dress. Yasmin offered to help edit the entire video together, with the help of her mom, who was a graphic designer for a big company and knew all about video editing. And Khalamoni said she'd oversee everything—with Adam as her assistant.

"What about me?" Nadia asked. She was the only person still without a job.

"You'll be the interviewer, obviously," Khalamoni said with a smile. There was a mischievous twinkle in her eye, like she had known all along this would be Nadia's job but had wanted to keep it a surprise until Nadia asked.

"I'll be the interviewer?" Nadia asked, astonished. "But . . . I've never interviewed anyone before. You're the journalist!"

"I can help you if you want, but, Nadia, you've spent most of this summer with me, talking to Reem, talking to the women at the shelter. You've even been writing about everything you've learned. And Reem trusts you, probably more than she trusts me!" Khalamoni said. "You're the best person to interview her, and you're already an amazing journalist. I know you can do it."

Nadia wasn't so sure, but if Khalamoni believed in her then she had to believe in herself too.

"Okay," Nadia said. "I'll do it!"

The day of the video shoot arrived, and Nadia was nervous. Her stomach felt like butterflies were fluttering around everywhere! She didn't like the feeling, but when Khalamoni greeted her that morning with a smile, some of Nadia's nervousness disappeared. She and Khalamoni had worked hard to make sure that Nadia was asking all the right questions.

Everyone piled into Mama and Mami's car and made the drive to Reem's village. That was the first portion of their video. They filmed the streets of Bangladesh, the drive into the village, and what the village looked like. They even passed by some areas that were flooded and caught it on camera.

Outside Reem's house, Nadia and Reem sat side

by side under the lights and the camera. Nadia thought it would feel uncomfortable with so many people around them. But they were all friends and family, including Reem and her parents, so it didn't feel strange at all.

She turned to the camera and began the introduction she and Khalamoni had planned out.

"Hi, everyone. I'm Nadia Islam! I'm eight years old, and I came to Bangladesh with my family to celebrate my summer vacation. And when I came here, I learned a lot about Bangladesh. I learned about what my city, Sylhet, looks like. I learned about all the amazing street food here. I learned about how Bangladesh has almost eight hundred rivers! And . . . when I met my friend Reem, I learned about climate change and how that has been affecting Bangladesh. So, I wanted everyone to know about what I learned in Bangladesh this summer."

Nadia turned to Reem, who smiled brightly.

"Reem, can you tell us about who you are and what you do?"

"Hi, Nadia," said Reem. "Yes, I'm Reem Talukdar and I'm twelve years old! I've lived in Bangladesh my whole life. I live in a village in Sylhet city with my family, but a few years ago a terrible flood washed away a lot of the houses in my village. My parents and I were lucky because our house is at the top of a hill. We left our house behind when the floods were at their worst and went to live with family we had in Dhaka. Thankfully, our house was okay, but not everyone was so lucky. After that, I decided to learn more about why the floods happen here so often, and I was surprised by what I found."

"What did you find?" Nadia asked.

"Well . . . I found out that Bangladesh is a country really vulnerable to climate change effects, and that our coastal areas, the areas around the sea, are slowly going underwater. A lot of people live in those areas, and as more time goes by, more and more of those people are left without houses. They're completely displaced."

"That's horrible!" Nadia said.

Reem nodded somberly. "I know. And it's all because Bangladesh is on low-lying land. It's the same reason why we have all of these floods. When we have heavy rain, our rivers overflow and they flood everything. Villages and cities, farmland . . . so much is destroyed, and so many people lose everything!"

"What can we do about it?" Nadia asked.

"We have to find a long-term solution to stop the floods and stop our land from going underwater. But we can also help in small ways. My family and I helped by making a shelter for women and children in one of the highest areas in Sylhet, where we hope no floodwater will go. We take people there so they have a place to stay, and we help them get back on their feet," Reem said.

Everyone applauded as Reem and Nadia finished up their interview. Nadia felt her heart fill with pride. She couldn't believe she had done it—she had interviewed someone like a real-life journalist, and it had felt easy. It had even felt fun!

"You're a really good interviewer," Reem said as they started packing up their things to visit the shelter for the last part of their video.

"You're a really good interviewee!" said Nadia.

Eid Mubarak!

By the time the entire video was filmed and edited by Yasmin, it was the last day of Ramadan. Nadia could hardly believe an entire month had passed by in the blink of an eye.

"What are we going to do for Eid tomorrow?" Nadia asked Ammu. She had never spent an Eid in Bangladesh before.

"Your nanu bought new clothes for all of you," Ammu said. "Adam, your abbu and mama will go to the mosque for Eid prayer while we all get ready. And then they'll come home, and we'll have Eid breakfast."

"Just like at home!" Nadia said.

"Yes, but there are so many people here, I think

it'll be a busy day of people visiting us and us visiting people," Ammu said.

Nadia couldn't wait. An entire day of family, friends, and good food. This might end up being the best Eid ever.

Nadia knew she was right in her thinking when Yasmin sent her an email that night to say the video was ready.

"Everyone, come see the video!" Nadia called. They all shuffled in almost immediately, whispering excitedly to each other. She couldn't believe they had really pulled it off.

"Ready?" Nadia asked once everyone had gathered around.

"Ready!" Khalamoni said on everyone's behalf. Nadia hit play.

The video wasn't long—only ten minutes. But it was perfect. First, there was Nadia and Reem's interview. Then shots of the shelter, of the areas that were still flooded, and then the statistics that Khalamoni had researched to write her article, along with how they could donate to help the shelter and where they could learn more about climate change and Bangladesh. Finally, the video ended on photos of Reem, the shelter, and the people there that Khalamoni's friend had taken for her original article.

"Should we post it?" Nadia asked, looking around at her family.

"Let's post it tomorrow. On Eid day," Khalamoni said.

"Why on Eid?" Nadia asked.

"Because Eid is about celebration but also about giving, generosity," Khalamoni said.

"Really?" Nadia asked. She had always thought Eid was about new clothes and food. Every Eid Nadia got a brand-new dress and Ammu made enough food to feed an entire village.

"Yes. Do you know why we call it Eid al-Fitr?" Khalamoni asked.

Nadia shook her head.

"Because before Eid al-Fitr, all Muslims who can

support themselves have to pay something called a fitrana," Khalamoni said.

"What's that?" Nadia asked.

"It's a charitable donation we have to make," Khalamoni said. "So, you see . . . celebrating Eid encourages all of us to be charitable. To look out for one another. To support those who may be struggling."

"Because of something like a flood?" Nadia asked.

"Exactly," said Khalamoni.

On Eid morning, Nadia woke up feeling excited. It was strange to not be fasting anymore, but she knew that she would be keeping even more fasts the next year—without any kind of a Ramadan race needed!

Nadia put on the brand-new dress Nanu bought her. It was a pink-and-white salwar kameez that had sparkles. Nadia loved sparkles!

"Eid Mubarak!" Adam said. He was wearing new

clothes too: a black-and-white panjabi.

"Eid Mubarak!" Nadia said, hugging Adam tight.

"Eid Mubarak!" It was Lily and Rosie who said it next. They wore salwar kameezes with the same design as Nadia, but in different colors. Rosie was in red and white, and Lily was in orange and white. Nanu had picked out all of their clothes.

Nadia hugged the two of them too. During Eid you did a special hug. You hugged everyone twice, once on each side.

Nadia celebrated Eid with what seemed like the whole of Bangladesh. Every few minutes, the bell would ring and a new person would come running in with a box of mishtis or a dish with homemade food.

Nadia didn't mind! She ate all the delicious food and all of her favorite mishtis, she played games with Adam, Lily, and Rosie, and she didn't think about the Ramadan race even once.

"How do you think our video is doing?" Adam

asked in the evening when the festivities had died down a little bit.

"I haven't checked. Let's check now. I'll call Yasmin too!" Nadia sent a video call to Yasmin and she picked up quickly.

"Eid Mubarak!" Yasmin said as soon as she saw Nadia on her screen.

"Eid Mubarak!" Nadia, Adam, Lily, and Rosie all called back.

"What did you do for Eid?" Yasmin asked.

"So much!" Nadia said. "There were so many people celebrating here with us. What did you do?"

"We've barely even begun celebrating!" Yasmin said. "Eid only just started here. But I wore my new dress and I went to the mosque for Eid prayer."

Nadia missed spending Eid with Yasmin, but she knew that next year she would remember this Eid she spent in Bangladesh and miss spending Eid with her family.

"How is our video doing?" Adam asked.

"Hmm, I'm not sure . . ." said Yasmin. She furrowed her eyebrows together as she went to look. Suddenly, her eyes widened. "Over ten thousand views!"

"Wow!" Nadia said. She couldn't believe it. Ten thousand people had already watched the video. She tried to imagine ten thousand people coming into their house to celebrate Eid with them—it would be impossible! But by watching the video, it was almost like they had.

"Nadia, you're like a real-life journalist now," Yasmin said.

Nadia giggled. She knew there was more to journalism than interviewing her friend on video, but it was still nice to feel like a real journalist. "I guess. What's more important is that people are finally listening to Reem and what she has to say."

"And that people know about what's happening in Bangladesh," Rosie said.

"And that hopefully, people will be generous

and help," added Nadia. There was nothing more important than generosity when it came to Ramadan and Eid and being Muslim. Nadia knew that now.

NADIA ISLAM'S FACTS ABOUT CLIMATE CHANGE IN BANGLADESH (WITH STATISTICS FROM NADIA'S KHALAMONI)

#1: Bangladesh is one of the most climate-change vulnerable countries in the world! That's really scary because the whole *world* is affected by climate change, but Bangladesh might feel the effects before a lot of other countries.

#2: Scientists estimate that by the year 2050, one in seven people in Bangladesh will be displaced by climate change. That is a lot of people. Even people I know could be displaced!

#3: Because of the flooding and rising sea levels, over ten million people are already climate refugees in Bangladesh!

#4: Ms. Johnson said that burning fossil fuels (which is *not* renewable energy) produces greenhouse gases, like CO_2, which are bad for our environment. The average Bangladeshi person only produces 0.5 metric tons of CO_2, but the average person from the US produces 15.2 metric tons. But it's Bangladesh that's being hit much harder by climate change!

#5: We all need to work together for long-term solutions to climate change, in Bangladesh and across the world. But while we work on that, we can also help in small ways. Like helping climate refugees who are displaced in Bangladesh!

Nadia Goes Home

"Nadia, are you ready?" Ammu called from the other room. It was the week after Eid and almost time for Nadia and her family to go back home. Nadia quickly zipped up her suitcase. It was even more full than when she had come to Bangladesh. Before, it had only had Nadia's clothes, but now it had all of the gifts that she had been given during her time here. Lily and Rosie gave Nadia packs of their favorite Bengali candies. Nanu bought her another salwar kameez that sparkled. Mami gifted her a brand-new backpack, and Mama bought her a mug with Bengali words written on it. Nadia loved her gifts, but she could barely fit them all into her suitcase.

"Nadia!" Ammu called again.

"Coming!" said Nadia. She finished zipping up the suitcase and rushed out of the bedroom and toward the sitting room.

She was surprised to see Reem sitting on one of the couches, drinking some lemonade. She and Reem had been emailing back and forth, but Reem hadn't said anything about coming over!

"Reem!" Nadia said.

"Nadia, assalam alaikum," said Reem.

"Walaikum salam." Nadia sat down on one of the empty couches.

"I wanted to say goodbye before your flight tomorrow," Reem said.

"Oh . . ." Nadia said. She wished she didn't have to say goodbye. She hated saying goodbye, she had decided.

"And to give you this." Reem took something from her bag and held it out to Nadia. It was a tiny boat, just like the ones Nadia had seen around the rivers in Sylhet. "It's not much, but I

wanted to give you something to remember your summer here."

"I love it!" Nadia said. And it was just small enough to fit into her suitcase without any problems. She took the gift from Reem before standing up and pulling her into a big hug. "I'm glad we're friends, Reem, and I'm going to miss you."

"Me too," said Reem, sounding sad.

"But we can still keep in touch!" Nadia said. "And I can still help with your work here."

"Really?" Reem asked.

"Really!" said Nadia.

The next morning, Nadia had to wake up bright and early for the flight back home. She rubbed sleep out of her eyes and got dressed. When she and Adam dragged their suitcases outside, she saw that everyone was awake, even though it was six a.m.! Lily, Rosie, Mama, Mami, Nanu . . . they all looked just as tired as Nadia felt. They all looked just as sad too.

Nadia hugged everyone one at a time. First Mami, then Nanu, then Lily, and finally . . .

Rosie pulled her into the tightest hug of them all. "Sorry about all the Ramadan race stuff. You'll come back another summer, right?"

"Yes!" said Nadia, even though she was being squeezed to death. "And you have to come visit too."

"I will!" Rosie grinned after they had pulled apart.

Nadia and her family piled into Mama's car again. Nadia waved at everyone through the window, already missing them and already missing Bangladesh. She watched Sylhet city pass by the window as the car drove on. She watched the rickshaws and CNGs and cars and all the shops she was now familiar with. She didn't feel like she did when they had first come; she almost felt like she was leaving behind a second home.

"When can we come back to Bangladesh?" Nadia asked, turning to Ammu. "Next summer?"

Ammu chuckled. "Maybe, we'll see."

That didn't sound like a promise, but Nadia would take it!

A BRILLIANT BANGLADESHI SUMMER!

Written by Nadia Islam (editor in chief)
with art by Yasmin Oyeyemi

This summer, I went to Bangladesh with my family. At first, I wasn't excited about spending a summer there—I had never been to Bangladesh before, and I didn't know anybody there. But once I got there, everything changed. I met my family and even got the chance to help my aunt with her journalism. She was writing about climate change in Bangladesh, something I knew nothing about.

I ended up learning a lot. Not all of it was fun facts. I learned about flooding in Bangladesh and about how there are so many climate refugees there, and how there might be a lot more in the future!

At first, it made me feel scared and helpless. Climate change is such a big problem, and I am only eight years old. I'm not even a real journalist yet.

But then I realized that it doesn't matter that I'm only eight years old. My friend Reem was only ten when she learned about all of this stuff, and she decided that she would do whatever she could to help. When her village got flooded, and her neighbors lost everything, she and her family set up a shelter for them. They helped people who needed it the most, and they still help people who are affected by floods in Bangladesh.

Reem taught me how important it is for all of us to do what we can.

I learned a lot this summer: I learned about Ramadan, about Eid, about climate change. But maybe the most important thing I learned was that everyone—even someone as young as I am—can do something to create change.

Acknowledgments

This book was partly inspired by my own childhood, where I was lucky to grow up knowing many of my cousins. I have a lot of memories of getting up to mischief with my cousins, from when I was very young, up until pretty recently. So, I would like to thank my family for giving me that childhood, which not everyone is fortunate to have.

Thank you especially to my siblings, to whom this book is dedicated: Bhaiya and Labiba. Thank you also to my sister-in-law, Biyut apu. Thank you to all my cousins, but especially to Nazifa Nawal, Mira, Afrin, Fariha, Tahmid, Touqir, Samiyah, Iliyeen, and Faiza.

Thank you to my friends for all their support throughout the years, especially Gavin, Alyssa, Faridah, Tammi, Priyanka, Gayatri, Lia, and Ramona.

This book has had an interesting journey, and I know that it wouldn't have made it this far without my agent, Uwe Stender. Thank you for always being my number one advocate.

Making the jump from young adult to middle grade was a daunting task at times, but it was made easier with the help of my brilliant editor, Courtney Stevenson. Thank you for helping to shape this book into what it is today.

Thank you also to everyone on my publishing team for all of your hard work in getting this book out there: Kathryn Silsand, James Neel, Laura Mock, Alison Klapthor, and Emily Mannon.

Thank you to Avani Dwivedi for the beautiful cover art and interior illustrations.

Finally, thank you to you for picking up this book and giving it a chance.